'Most of What is Complete Waste

Monologues, Dialogues, Sketches and Other Writings

N.F. Simpson

edited by
David Crosher & Ian Greaves

This collection first published in 2013 by Oberon Books Ltd
521 Caledonian Road, London N7 9RH
Tel: +44 (0) 20 7607 3637 / Fax: +44 (0) 20 7607 3629
e-mail: info@oberonbooks.com
www.oberonbooks.com

A catalogue record for this book is available
from the British Library.

PB ISBN: 978-1-78319-023-2
E ISBN: 978-1-78319-522-0

Cover illustration by Patrick Hughes

Not Just Now, Thanks (p.83) by Les Coleman

Photograph on p.xxvi by Mike Harris

Material on pages 14, 32, 39, 45, 58, 67, 80, 86, 128, 136, 138, 144,
160 courtesy of Maurice Hatton, Willie Rushton and *Private Eye*

Printed, bound and converted
by CPI Group (UK) Ltd, Croydon, CR0 4YY.

In memory of Les Coleman

Contents

Introduction

by Simon Usher

> My plays are about life – life as I see it.
> (N.F. Simpson, *Why I Write* (1973))

> If you stuffed a ship full to bursting point with human bodies, there would be such loneliness that they would all freeze.
> (Bertolt Brecht, *In the Jungle of Cities* (1923))

The French novelist and playwright Marguerite Duras called life 'this reign of injustice'. The question of what you do about it concerns most of us. Duras's response was alcohol, imbibed on a daily basis. N.F. Simpson's was laughter, procured moment by moment to atone for the 'perfidy of getting born' (p.148).

Today, people believe that depression can be cured. Well, perhaps. But as Hamm the landowner in Beckett's *Endgame* (1957) observes, 'You're on earth, there's no cure for that!' Depression, though, can be the carrier of many other things; humour to name one, or exhilaration. It is as well to remember these dualisms when considering the case of N.F. Simpson, who stands in relation to Beckett in the same way as, say, Webster or Ford to Shakespeare; indebted, but radically new as well as somehow free of the burden of having to be great.

In *New Life* (2009; p.81), Mr Herbison answers an advertisement from an organisation which assesses your life by putting it through a computer. When the results have come in, a Mrs Yarmouth asks 'What's wrong with his life?' To which the official replies:

> It's what I would describe, in broad terms, Mrs Yarmouth, as ramshackle. One gets the impression of something just thrown together at random in an altogether amateurish way with very little thought as to what purpose it was ultimately intended to serve. How it has managed to keep going as a more or less viable entity for as long as it has is frankly something of a mystery.

Note the separation of the man from his life, like the Cheshire cat and its smile. The ramshackleness is the means by which this particular life has circumvented emergencies or catastrophe. Simpson is filtering his own autobiography through the operations of a bureaucratic, depersonalising system. This is a method you will see employed in numerous ways in this extraordinary selection. It is a selection at war with the useful, the utilitarian, the quotidian and the merely functional. If this suits your cast of mind, you will find much here to cheer you.

Those who 'reign' will not abdicate. In fact, the roots of their supposed entitlement extend ever deeper. As for the rest of us, we can decide only how we see them. Simpson takes up fresh vantage points with unfailing energy. It is no wonder binoculars or 'field glasses' figure prominently in his plays and prose. Windows too. Life is a game of perspective in which we all of us are engaged, whether willingly or not.

One perspective, though – the reverse in a sense – needs to be addressed at the outset. This is the regard in which Simpson himself is held. Surviving colleagues bridle at the idea of taking him too seriously. 'He would have hated it. He hated pretension,' they say. This is understandable, but it reflects an attitude which hasn't helped his reputation. He didn't want to be seen taking himself seriously: he was an impeccably modest man. But, as you will see from his superlative critical and self-critical writings, he did so himself, from time to time, while steadfastly maintaining a disinterested tone.

Simpson was a writer with definite philosophical proclivities, so couldn't live on irony alone. The English theatre establishment in general has an aversion to this kind of writing, except in its softer form where the audience is flattered into thinking it has an *a priori* knowledge and understanding of some well-known but complex political or scientific question. There are no such givens in Simpson's dramatic explorations. Had he been French he may well have been seen by now in the class of Perec or Queneau. In *Species of Spaces and Other Pieces* (1974, translated 1997), Perec asks 'What does it mean to live in a room?' Among his propositions are: 'Is it when you've used up all the non-matching hangers in the cupboard? Is it when you've drawing-pinned to the wall an old postcard showing Carpaccio's *Dream of St Ursula*? Is it when you've experienced there the throes of anticipation, or the exultations of passion, or the torments of a toothache?' These are questions which Simpson might well have asked in the interest of charging the random with an air of permanence, but things being as they are he is still waiting to be accorded his rightful place in the canon. All I will attempt to do here, following Randall Jarrell's example in *Some Lines from Whitman* (1953), is introduce you to his genius, as evidenced by these short plays, soliloquies, poems and essays.

I'll begin with a little personal history. I only knew N.F. 'Wally' Simpson in the last few years of his life but consider myself very lucky in this respect. *A Resounding Tinkle* (1957) was the second play scheduled for a public reading in the English Stage Company's Fiftieth Anniversary Programme at the Royal Court in 2006. Bill Gaskill, who'd directed the original production, was directing the reading, but, for various reasons unconnected to Simpson felt compelled to withdraw. Ian Rickson, the artistic director of the Royal Court, knew I was an admirer of Simpson's work and asked me to step into Gaskill's shoes. I was of course delighted, though slightly nervous about encountering the legendary and slightly mysterious Simpson in person. I was sure of one thing, though. I wanted to direct the original two-act version of the play, as opposed to the one-act version it was distilled to at the request of Tony Richardson and George Devine in 1957. Like most theatre directors of my now rapidly ageing generation I was in awe of the brilliant and redoubtable Gaskill, but felt confident enough in the worth of the full version to go ahead with it. I had, for instance, always been drawn to the melancholic and Beckettian bi-play of the two Comedians, shorn completely from the one-act version.

My route to Simpson was Beckett, but there was a difference. The parts of Simpson I liked were less solipsistic than Beckett; not in any way better, but perhaps allowing a little more chaos through. My attention to Beckett won out in my late teens, however. It was the criminally neglected playwright and fellow Beckett devotee David Drane, himself influenced by Simpson, who later recommended I read the plays more thoroughly. Wally had noted David's voice when he was Literary Manager at the Royal Court in the Seventies and passed on one of his plays to David Gothard, another friend, on the grounds that it was 'quite Polish'. (Drane is from Lowestoft and Gothard typically connected this Polishness to the fact that this is where Conrad first put in to an English harbour as a young seaman; an irony Wally would have enjoyed.) I read Simpson again in my early twenties and realised that I had been partly subject to a conventional view of the writer as a decidedly English satirist who belonged to the Fifties and Sixties. And this was despite my youthful attraction to the playful despair of the Comedians. It was the poetic red setters, Death's head and station lights in *One Way Pendulum* (1959) which now compelled my attention, as the forceps and boots had done in *Waiting for Godot* (1953).

So it was as a dramatic poet that I first really grasped Simpson's genius, and it is as such that I can at least partly recommend him to you as he appears in this selection. And of course, the best poetry is also the best philosophy.

My initial view of Simpson had been altered considerably and I knew I wanted to direct the plays. In reality I have been mostly thwarted in this respect, the more common responses from producers and artistic directors being 'I don't like absurdism' (a term Wally disliked), 'It's dated and it's not funny', 'I've never heard of him' (probably the most common) and 'Oh, I thought he was dead.'

Wally was delighted as well as encouraged by the reading of the two-act *Tinkle* at the Royal Court. The play's original design seemed vindicated. The audience, young and old, found it irresistibly funny. Wally was especially pleased that it was played straight and not for laughs, an oft-stated credo of his (of which more later). He rang me afterwards to tell me he'd woken in the night laughing out loud at those two fine actors, Alan Williams and the late Peter Sproule, who'd read the reinstated comedians.

This began a collaboration with Wally which has been one of the most important partnerships in my directing career. I went on to help him develop his final play *If So, Then Yes* (2010) but sadly the Royal Court could not see its way to staging a return by one of its greats in his eighties. It's ironic that they have since specifically invited playwrights in their eighties to submit plays, when they had a genius and one of their own right under their noses only a year or two before. Wally never learnt the art of self-promotion; he was much too nice a man to bother anyone with anything except his sheer merit.

What is the source of Simpson's remarkable, self-generating body of work? The simple answer is a linguistic and emotional tension which produces poetry. Orwell, in *Why I Write* (1946), says that 'before [the writer] ever begins to write he will have acquired an emotional attitude from which he will never completely escape.' Simpson, in his own essay *Why I Write* (p.147 –148), speaks of what it is:

> To feel personally responsible not only for every crime, every atrocity, every act of inhumanity that has ever been perpetrated since the world began, but for those as well that have not as yet been so much as contemplated, is something which only Jesus Christ and I can ever have experienced to anything like the same degree. And it goes a long way to account for what I write and why I write it. For not only must one do what one can by writing plays to make amends for the perfidy of getting born; one must also, in the interests of sheer self-preservation, keep permanently incapacitated by laughter as many as possible of those who would otherwise be the bearers of a just and terrible retribution. One snatches one's reprieve quite literally laugh by laugh.

Simpson's Baptist origins mark this passage. The sentiment seems positively Calvinist, except that *his* expiation will be through laughter rather than Divine Grace, although the two – grace and laughter – are more or less interchangeable in Simpson's universe. It is an attitude in Orwell's sense, too – a compulsion, an index for Simpson's quarrel with the world, for his amusement at human self-regard, pomposity and vanity. He, like all of humanity's best critics, is the worst sinner of all and his self-imposed means of redemption punishingly hard: to procure laughter in others on a regular basis, as Rosalind once bade Berowne do for a year, in a hospital for the terminally sick, to win her love in Shakespeare's *Love's Labour's Lost* (1598).

Laughter is grace. A tinkle resounds. Paradox is emphatically at the heart of Simpson's writing. Taken together, Bro and Middie *Paradock* in *A Resounding Tinkle* announce this loud and clear. So how does this connect to the 'emotional attitude'? I would describe it as something like an active reticence, or, as Simpson himself put it in *Why I Write*, 'a love of order tempered by a deep and abiding respect for anarchy'. A surrender to flux, to the fact that every attitude co-exists with its exact opposite, is one part of Simpson's stance. Why become involved in the destructive game of human life when the basis for it is self-evidently unstable and delusional? Simpson, though, was always a step away from his fellow Royal Court playwrights in the sense that he saw language at the root of this delusion, this human deluge of 'bad faith'. Quite an unusual view for our domestic dramatists and well ahead of its time. The English have never understood Beckett's modernism in this respect, preferring to nettle him in productions with stock characterisations; so what were Simpson's chances? Some critics took him to task for a lack of characterisation but character is inevitably quite a fluid concept in Simpson's universe. Language keeps getting in its way. There are human beings, or even 'souls', in Simpson's plays and prose. They exist, however, as actual people do, in the gaps between moments of stability and immanence. You *can* hear their cries, louder even than Jimmy Porter's.

The trouble for Simpson – a would-be Humanist – is that we humans have a very high opinion of ourselves. We can't or won't reconcile ourselves to the tragic insignificance of our place in the universe. Given our true circumstances it is remarkable how rooted so many feel in the social narrative constructed for them, particularly when you consider how threadbare the social contract has become and how unfashionable self-sacrifice, regardless of the pointlessness or sanctity of life, has grown. Simpson enjoys no such certainty or rootedness, and indeed displays a hatred of the human hierarchies others defer to. He is aghast at how easily we are persuaded away from our natural responses and reactions. Chekhov was a master of human changeability in this respect. Think of the story in which a young writer sends his work off to a magazine and after two weeks receives a letter advising him to take up another profession. His girlfriend dismisses the editors as fools who know nothing, but, as the days pass, she begins to say that perhaps they have a point, that they must know what they're talking about. We tend to believe those in authority, even though we suspect that most of them cheated their way to it. 'A dog's obeyed in office', as King Lear observed. So, the reign of injustice is in our minds as much as in the external world. As a Catholic educated at a monastery school I can identify with Simpson's need to convert sin into a workable basis for action. But, as one learns from Beckett also, the sin of getting born is only the beginning of our troubles. Guilt is the master-light in Simpson. There is no lack of emotion in his work – often a criticism of comic drama – but rather too much. It must be hived off and distributed among a series of interrelated personae. There is something of the best English religious poetry in what one might call – echoing George Herbert – Simpson's militant reticence, a recoiling back to modesty in the face of injustice: 'I struck the board and cry'd, No more!'

The reined-in emotion – the Calvinism – sometimes escapes its bounds, however, as one of the most unusual and arresting short works here, the Chaplinesque *Window* (1974; p.149–151), attests. It is a pained little glance of a play, as delicate as its principal character Arnold's eyes are weak. We discover Arnold standing on a chair in his parents' living room trying to see to the other side of the road through the window, but he can see nothing. In this play we the audience see, as it were, the skull beneath the skin, the mound of garbage behind the gleaming rail of Simpson's language. The facade is smashed to admit a flood of anger. An obsession with money and 'getting on' manifests itself with terrible force. Arnold's mother laments the amount of cash they've spent on opticians for their chronically short-sighted son:

> MOTHER: We haven't begrudged what we've spent either. But it would be nice to have some kind of success to show for it.
>
> ARNOLD: I'm not responsible, am I, mother, for being short-sighted! I'm not short-sighted for fun!
>
> MOTHER: One only wishes one could be sure.
>
> FATHER: If you're not responsible for it, who, in heaven's name, is?
>
> MOTHER: Somebody else, presumably.

Perfect injustice! This is Ibsen in miniature; a four-act drama in three pages. We've all stamped our foot and protested 'I'm not short-sighted for fun!' or its equivalent. Who hasn't caustically proclaimed 'Somebody else, presumably' when applying the boot to a member of his own family? Arnold is being punished for 'the perfidy of getting born.' It's his lookout that he has crippling short-sight. '[You'll be] selling matches in the gutter, with twenty-nine or thirty children to support,' taunts his mother. English parents of the Victorian persuasion always see the worst possible consequences in their children's actions. Even as the sight-blighted and club footed Arnold leaves, having ground his glasses into the floor with his surgical boot, slammed the door behind him and crashed, near blind, down the stairs, his parents don't help. After all, it's his fault. His mother merely moves across to his father and asks, 'Where did we go wrong, James?' She means 'What aspect of his training did we neglect?'

As Bergson, the philosopher the Comedians cite in *A Resounding Tinkle*, and a key influence on Simpson, observes in *Laughter* (1900): 'Were man to give way to the impulse of his natural feelings, were there neither social nor moral law, these outbursts of violent feeling would be the ordinary rule of life.' For the most part we accept social and moral law, but deep within we know that such laws are ontological in nature and therefore fundamentally unchanging. They are, in Sartre's words, 'decisions about existence,' always made by *other* people. We shift from a violent anarchy to a sort of conditional acceptance, although the nihilistic individualism of our age means we think less and less about it anyway.

So, at the heart of this collection is a window through which you see nothing, in a room where you are barely tolerated. Try to escape and you smash your ineffectual glasses and crash down the stairs. These children are their parents' enemies, with the mother or father proclaiming 'you're ruining our lives with your impossible behaviour! Leave us alone!' Simpson continually shows us how an immutable and self-perpetuating form of authority operates in adulthood as well, compelling many of us to remain virtual children mostly against our will. We see this relationship in the longer of the two poems in this volume, *One of Our St Bernard Dogs is Missing* (1977/1982; p.113–116). It is a Brechtian parable which demonstrates how we collaborate in our own oppression by others, as we have been trained to. A man who has struggled through the snow to find shelter is at the door of a monastery.

A moot point
Whether I was going to
Make it.

I just had the strength
To ring the bell.

One of the monks inside eventually responds to his ringing
and opens the door, but far from welcoming him, as you would
expect a monk to do, he suggests, cunningly, that the man go
back out into the snow to find a St Bernard Dog which has gone
missing and is presumed lost. At one point he produces a flask of
whisky and gives it to the man, who has accepted that the monk's
proposal makes 'a kind of sense', since he is already out in the
cold:

What is it?
I said
It's a flask
He said
Of brandy.
Ah
I said.

For the dog
He said.

Good thinking
I said.

The monk possesses a jocular, monastic persona, but he is
actually a calculating and vicious figure. Yet the man is duly
respectful. This is the Brechtian ingredient. The man doesn't
see the human being in front of him, only the monk. He is in
fact too polite to separate the two. The monk – this particular
monk – knows this is the case, so he is able to usurp the man's
co-operative and subservient spirit for his own selfish purpose,
to remain in the warmth of the monastery, to send someone
to whom he should be extending charity packing. Perhaps, we
suspect, there is no St Bernard dog missing at all, which would
only deepen the monk's calumny.

This is a method Simpson employs frequently. He sets a
'melodic line', to use his formula from *Making Nonsense of Nonsense*
(1966; p.69–79), to establish a character's *master* attitude, but
this line is contradicted by what is actually being said. This is
how power is exercised in life. The one thing social convention

forbids you to do, however, is to become visibly upset when on the receiving end.

The drill
He said
When you find it
If you ever do
Is to lie down.

Right
I said
Will do.
Lie down on top of it
He said

The man goes off, but, after a week, he still doesn't know where 'to start getting down to looking.' He has frostbite and – that inextinguishable heartbeat of human beings – hope. That is all.

We mostly capitulate. We store our rage away for another day, a day which for most of us never comes, owing to death, disease or a frank loss of faculties. Yet we are still ready to believe those in a cloak of authority, and this authority is often inscribed in their language. Simpson saw the ebbing of language, from its revelatory potential, to providing a mere screen behind which officials and bureaucrats can hide. His work is diagnostic in this respect.

There is not much appetite in society, or indeed in the theatre, to develop an antidote or prescribe a cure for the damaged span of our language. Those who resist like the Comedians are extremists too singular to engage with the mass. Hud and Crob in *Can You Hear Me?* (1959; p.15–20) are still trying. Hud likes shouting down an ear trumpet with other enthusiasts in a hotel once or twice a week, while Crob is intent on listening to other people's conversations through a speaking tube from their room. Hud orders a tube for Crob on the way down to his ear trumpet gathering and a bellboy duly brings one to the room. Crob cannot close the door because of the length of tube extending through it, the end of which he is already holding to his ear. '*He listens for a moment with all the rapture of an addict*' before adapting the speaking tube to become first a shower head and then a sun-ray lamp – which eventually detonates – while listening all the while to conversations from another part of the hotel. This physical anarchist, taking the long way round in his dogged battle with the utility of objects, will appear throughout the present volume in a variety of guises. 'Why can't you shout down an ear trumpet like anybody else?' observes one of the people he's been listening in to after the detonation.

This play, grounded in the Beckettian 'marriage' of Hud and Crob (how and why they booked into a hotel room together we do not know) transmits the pure joy of men-in-the-world-with-objects. Which, the man or the object, is ultimately the *thing*? Relationships between human beings in Simpson are generally a sort of dance in which one party tries to objectify the other. The monk in *One of Our St Bernard Dogs is Missing* makes his visitor a *thing*. If we think of Brecht's formula of 'a' and 'the', we are all of us struggling to be THE monk rather than A monk. In *Can You Hear Me?* Crob is struggling to stay in command of an actual *thing*, the speaking tube, and is in truth failing to do so. The stage direction '*with all the rapture of an addict*' – an extraordinary piece of direction, forensically precise – calls to mind Brecht's 'inductive method' of acting in which you objectify the gesture, enabling the audience to resist the actor's will to subjectivity. Simpson often cited Bergson's suggestion that the reception of comedy requires 'a momentary anaesthesia of the heart', followed by a reflux of pity for Man's condition.

The comedy in Simpson is wired to the *experience* of living; to what it's *like* being a man or a woman in the world. The theatre allows language, the body and objects to collide with maximum force. Weighty things – moments of living and dying, time, distance – fly about the stage with the lightness and speed of spinning tops, rather like the heart, liver and lungs in 16th Century monastic illustrations of the warring humours. What is the relationship between our own consciousness of self and the phenomena (other people and objects) we confront? As the narrator of Beckett's *Texts for Nothing* (1950-52) ruefully observes, there are always 'other others.' For Simpson, as for Beckett, this problem begins closer to home, before you even consider the *world* that is another person. In our own mouth, for example.

In *Anyone's Gums Can Listen to Reason* (1977; p.7–13) – a nice, provocative title – the matter is teeth, a recurring preoccupation in Simpson. Set in a simple Quaker Meeting Hall, this miniature masterpiece establishes three young people – Steve, Harriet and

Frances – sitting silently at the pews, before Harriet softly and unemphatically starts telling the story of a man, Murgatroyd, whose gums have gone on strike and evicted his teeth: 'There was a sound like small marbles dropping on to the floor...some twenty or thirty of them...' After talking about Murgatroyd's teeth for a period, in Quaker mode, the three younger people withdraw into a meditative silence, '*tuned in to eternity*' while three older people start to reflect, as if '*in a waiting room*', on the trials and tribulations humans face in housing their teeth and gums. Teeth caught in a misalliance with the gums have ideas of their own: '[Galileo's] incisors were as likely as not wandering hand-in-hand through some meadow or other picking daisies.' The relationship can, however, be a happy one. The man whose gums are 'pulling their weight' is a happy man: 'All the teeth working harmoniously together – hand in glove – for the good of the whole organism.' When the older people retire into their own silence, the younger ones speak up again:

STEVE: All Mr Murgatroyd's teeth were by this time gathered up and handed back.

HARRIET: 'What are we going to do with them?' asked Mrs Pertwee, ever practical.

FRANCES: 'I've got a matchbox.' he said. 'They can go in there.'

Pause.

HARRIET: But, search as he would through all his pockets, no matchbox could be found.

STEVE: It was the work, however, of a moment to drop the teeth into his pocket.

FRANCES: Where they remained.

Pause.

This is Simpson at his sublime best. Mediating the story through the melodic line of a Quaker meeting – voices coming and going – allows the play its characteristic doubleness: at once, divine grace and 'mechanical inelasticity'. At the close, in a moment of virtual dream play, Harriet describes Murgatroyd 'slipping his teeth back in one at a time', as chaos is once again momentarily stabilised and the man is put back together again. This is something like magic realism; Simpson via Borges and Perec.

The difficulties of being in the world become more diffuse even than the perambulations of Murgatroyd's teeth, as this passage from *"I Know It's Not"* (2009; p.53) suggests:

> I know it's not a fashionable thing to say these days, but you don't have to go far to see the hoof of a Dartmoor pony imprinted on most of your present-day crimes.

Why should this proposition *not* be true? After all, a government's decision to bomb another country is often made on the grounds of a proposition founded on *apparent* logic and reason. Yet there is often no more sense to it than the appearance of a Dartmoor pony's hoofmark on the Marie Celeste. Like death, a pony's hoofmark gets everywhere.

And what about Galashiels? For every person "*Due in Galashiels*" (2009; p.100), billions are not. But if you a person who is due in the town of Galashiels, then, of course, it is the middle of the world:

> And yet, when you come down to it, there must be a whole host of people who've gone through their entire lives without ever having been due in Galashiels at all!

Think of *them*, Simpson's representative is urging, if the thought of being due in Galashiels runs away with you! Both Galashiels and the pony's hoofmarks exist in our minds as much as in physical reality. For most of us, *our* house is THE house because we spend most of our time in it. But for visitors it exists only marginally and not at all for the billions of others who have never seen or been inside it. Simpson insists on viewing us in the correct scale and perspective.

The plays and other works here counsel us against any form of reliance on givens, which are delusional as a rule. Simpson's mock- or anti-'heroic' characters can't rest on their laurels. Whatever they do must be undertaken with vigour and commitment, even when they are compelled to take the *very* long way round. The *Twins* (2010; p.137) resemble one another every day. They actually have to get on and *resemble* one another. It's 'going on all the time'. This is a commendable stance in Simpson's universe, to avoid the fixed if you can see your way to doing so: 'I am wondering if I should take up Morris dancing,' says one of his militantly reticent monologuists (*Snippets*, 1982; p.130–133). Why not? Many of the figures in these pages are cautious existentialists. The world refuses time and again to respond to our perfectly logical and reasonable expectations of it. Yet we must at all costs avoid 'the dreadful and destructive ravages of that most terrible of all known forms, which goes by the name of sanity' (p.79). To claim sanity is to participate in the delusion. Ear trumpets, Tube stations, hoofmarks, teeth: 'all things flow,' as Heraclitus said. The drive to impose order is ever-present, but is it wise? One of Simpson's masters, J.B.S. Haldane, could say of the Creator only that he had 'an inordinate fondness for beetles.' Perspective again. Is it terrifying or liberating to imagine that a tadpole could be exchanged for a human being with no significant loss of value? Simpson himself claims to have taken life 'very much as it comes' (p.158).

Yet, amid the flow, there persists in Simpson a deep belief in, or rather a need to believe in, a Creator, a Designer, a Prime Mover; a wish to engage via his characters in a dialogue with such a Being. The speaker of *God's Whippet* (1983/2006; p.48) comments on St Thomas Aquinas, 'he was unwise even to contemplate proving the existence of God but, to my mind, it is a measure of the man that, notwithstanding the risks, he was ready to have a go.' Be a Doubting Thomas then, but don't, like Richard Dawkins, rule God's existence out. Conceit is the enemy of thought. Like St Thomas Aquinas, we lack the means to imagine a dimension in which God *could* exist; all we can do is stop our impulse to rationalise getting in the way of our relation to the world as it *is*. Better to leave things alone. As Simpson's great Romanian precursor Ionesco insisted, 'A tree doesn't need permission to be a tree.' Yet man has settled nihilistically for consciousness consisting in what he consumes. Simpson's work absolutely refuses to accept this decline in our perception. He isn't a passive writer in that respect. Indeed, as far back as *The Hole* (1958) you can detect an anger lurking near the comic surface.

A large number of his characters or personae find life baffling as well as difficult. They can't secure an angle from which to approach it. They find themselves in a constant process of arriving at and disappearing from self, often by the most convoluted means; hence the binoculars. 'If only I could get closer to life!', they are saying. Language itself often overwhelms them, curated and administered as it is by authority in one form or another. According to Sartre, 'we are condemned to be free.' Yes, and in the best of all possible worlds!

Here is Simpson's interviewer in the stringent self-examination *Making Nonsense of Nonsense* (1966), reflecting on their dialogue:

> As we chatted it soon became apparent that, for what it was worth, Mr Simpson's opinion of God was not all that much higher than his opinion of Man. When I asked him why he nevertheless continued to believe, unlike so many of his contemporaries, in the existence of a Supreme Being, his reply was simple and to the point. Who else, he said, could have boobed on that kind of scale? (p.72)

In other words, *Mr* Simpson is suggesting that God cannot have intended the universe to turn out the way it did – it wasn't his design, yet no one else had the wherewithal to try. He had a go – and we owe our existence to His efforts – but, in the final analysis, He possibly lacked the know-how to pull it off with complete success, which is forgivable really, given the scale of the work. Simpson had a rare ability to write seriously about religion in a comic vein. The Baptist, the spiritualist in him, mitigates the satirist's gesture. There is prudence in his penetrating phrases and sentences, a reticence corrected by a will to rhetorical extravagance. He writes of the obligation 'to recognise, before it's too late, the one paramount need – which is to cut ourselves down to size' (p.74). The key here is 'before it's too late.' How urgent this is in a period of riotous self-inflation. The Established Church is like the monk in *One of Our St Bernard Dogs is Missing* writ large. The media imposes on us what Simpson in *World in Ferment* (1969; p.156–159) calls 'the illusion of being in the know.' We need to sympathise with God as He surveys the wreckage of His plans. After all, the beauty and poise of animals and trees remain. He got some of it right. Simpson's militant reticence is a valuable weapon for conscience and consciousness amid the dumb noise of humanity in the developed world.

It *is* disappointing when we realise that life, society, is a 'reign of injustice' and in plain sight of a putative Supreme Being. It is yet again a question of perspective, though. Simpson describes Man as the 'seeing animal' (*New Left Review* interview, July/

August 1961). This is our blessing and our curse because, unless corrected, this 'sight' tends to narcissism, to dumb noise and a lack of perspective. Merleau-Ponty is useful here: 'Visible and mobile, my body is a thing […] But, because it moves itself and sees, it holds things in a circle around itself.' Man can see but he is perpetually constricted by his physical limits. Technology has hardened this wall around the self – this illusion – and removed many of the barriers to treating others as things, as mere objects. What we forget, from this throne of false subjectivity, is that we ourselves are *things*. Think of watching a large group of people engaged, ant-like, in a repetitive activity. How easy it is to objectify them, to see them as determined only by what they are *doing*. The 'seeing animal' will become the 'doing animal', but in the moment of *seeing* he does not think he will. You begin to understand how the serial killer and St Francis are interchangeable in Simpson's reality. The 'seeing animal' is now dominant, marking out the subject territory for which we are all of us fighting as individuals. The essay *World in Ferment* is prophetic in this respect. Here (with my emphasis), Simpson is commenting on the reaction to *Cathy Come Home*, Jeremy Sandford's 1966 television play which highlighted the plight of the homeless:

> Could there have been a single publication anywhere for months afterwards which did not carry some expression of outraged indignation, some fierce, well-merited denunciation of some authority or other, some clarion call to action on the part of *almost anybody* but *the writer*.

Simpson goes on to say that we have flattered our ego 'by enormously enlarging the scale on which we nowadays imagine we are operating.' And he wrote this in the Sixties! After all, these symptoms gave way to the actual disease some years ago. At least Hud wanted to shout down something and Crob to listen through another thing (while performing his singular contortions at the same time). There is a negotiation. When interviewed by BBC Radio for the opening of the film version of *One Way Pendulum* in 1965, Simpson suggested that, far from witnessing the fracturing of communication, we may have been mistaken about its nature all along:

> It isn't so much about a failure to communicate, as a discovery in the last thirty years that communication is no longer the

same thing that we'd always imagined it to be. In fact, when we're talking we're not exchanging ideas or information, or rather that this is not the only way of communicating; that you can communicate simply by making noises. The very fact that two people are talking at cross-purposes but are making noises is a sort of recognition on the part of each of them that the other one is present in the room.

The individual is isolated and yet dependent on the 'other' to recognise himself as real. So the utter selfishness of our present individualism is a serious error. It is hardly surprising that some of Simpson's physical anarchists adopt a radical and difficult path. They are in search of the *real*.

> Each night I set my alarm clock by listening for the click and working the whole thing out from first principles because both the hands have come off, and each morning my day begins with a triumph for empiricism.
> (*Not Just Now, Thanks*, 1953; p.83-85)

So 'seeing' and 'doing' are to some extent rebalanced by the efforts of those who refuse to be the facile judges of others. This is revolution today. Bergson, the anatomist of 'mechanical inelasticity' – when we are given to ourselves as objects – paradoxically said that 'we cannot become thoroughly acquainted with anything but our own heart.' You would hope that Arnold's parents in *Window* will eventually see themselves in their son, who is not unlike the donkey in Robert Bresson's *Au Hasard Balthasar* (1966): passive, defenceless and vulnerable, fit only to receive and encourage the blows and taunts of others, but interchangeable, ultimately, with the youth who ties a firework to his tail.

The 'seeing animal' is also the only animal capable of self-loathing. Had Simpson dwelt on this fact he may have written tragedy or its equivalent. Comedy requires innocence and who is to say this is not the truer and better part of us? Some years ago I picked up a copy of the Directors' Guild of Great Britain newsletter (a quixotic publication if ever there was one), in which a contributor had written of how 'senior members of the Guild have been running around like chickenless heads.' Whatever the origin of the mistake, it draws attention to the material nature of the metaphor it violates, making Guild members seem even more like things than the correct version would have done. I still wake in the night laughing at it and the laughter is heartless and cruel. Yet somehow as they are rendered ridiculous they become more human – their conceit pierced – as do I, the one seized with laughter, the 'seeing animal', when left less than proud of my own mirth.

Here, on the other hand, is a man who would rather not be made a fool of:

> What do you expect to be doing on eighteenth of February next?
>
> Well…
>
> Round the corner for a pound of best butter, perhaps.
>
> Something of that order…yes…it's quite a possibility.
>
> And then down to the coast for a quick dip in the briny before giving a lick of paint to the side of the garage no doubt.
>
> Yes, I wouldn't be at all surprised if that were not the scenario on the day in question.
>
> (*Prediction*, 2009; p.123)

Fear, death, uncertainty, hope: all are present in this tiny work. Which brings us to the question of construction. Simpson has been wrongly taken to task by critics for a weakness of structure in his dramatic work. The major plays have plots with spine – despite their discursiveness at times – whereas the works in this volume constitute more of a variegated and continuous act of dramatic creation. Intelligent, fluid, responsive actors will take to it. The canopy is exquisite, a machine of the articulate, the abortive emotions Jacobean or Restoration in scale.

Actors with good sense know that they mustn't try to be funny in Simpson. One must bite on the sentence or phrase. Become what the line makes you. Allow the thought its shape and integrity, however recondite or unlikely it is. Do not judge the thought in terms of your own reason, logic or 'sanity'. Woman 2 in *Escape* (1972; p.40–42) proclaims that 'The only reason [Yehudi Menuhin] plays the violin is to try and prove to the world that he's not a window cleaner.' This may or may not be true, but the actress in rehearsing the line comes to believe it. Or rather, the woman she is presenting must do so. Simpson performances in which the comedy is treated like a madcap version of sitcom are doomed. Wally wrote for actors. He knew they could effect the transfusion required to give life to lines 'coaxed out of the permanently undercharged batteries I was issued with at birth' (p.147), just as if they were the most normal things in the world to say – like Humphrey's breezy 'Be sensible' to Laura when she questions the painter Graham's insistence on working, like the man in *Not Just Now, Thanks,* from first principles for his portrait of Colonel Padlock in *Oh* (1960; p.96–99). Their obsession with Graham and the frequent repetition of his name has already converted them into virtual physical adjuncts of the painter, into *things*; thus, Laura is already rendered *insensible* when Humphrey makes his injunction to her to *be sensible*. 'You know Graham as well as I do, my dear. He doesn't often do things by halves.'

In light of this, it seems remarkably churlish of John Russell Taylor to have written in *Anger and After* (1963), 'Whether one likes or dislikes N.F. Simpson's work, it seems to me there is very little to say about it.' A comparison with Harold Pinter is instructive here. It is a sadness that Simpson's reputation suffered so badly in comparison with the younger man's, given that their reputations were formed at roughly the same time. (In fact, Pinter was an understudy on the original production of *The Hole*.) You can almost imagine Wally's Spooner to Pinter's Hirst in the mighty *No Man's Land* (1974) – the successful career writer tearing strips off a man he may once have known who is also a writer, but one who has fallen on hard times, if he ever flourished. Which is the happier? Spooner with his young devotees, or Hirst the chronic alcoholic, living behind drawn curtains in his Hampstead mansion? In a sense – and you will notice it in this volume – Wally's plays have things in common with Pinter's, but they lack the cruelty, the suave brutality of the victor's crowing. It is almost as if they have passed beyond it.

While Wally disappeared on the canals of England for twelve years, already well into late middle age, Pinter steamed ahead with his career as an all-round theatre man at the heart of the Establishment. It wasn't Wally's metier. He needed to spend time with people outside the cultural dragnet. He is temperamentally on the side of those being shafted. Pinter is too, but he was in a class of his own when writing those doing the shafting, as the tiny masterpiece *One For The Road* (1984) demonstrates. What they do share is a particular brand of stubborn melancholy, which was apparent one afternoon in 2006 when they met once more, briefly, at the Royal Court. Pinter was rehearsing *Krapp's Last Tape* (1958) and Wally attending rehearsals for a reading of his final play, *If So, Then Yes*. Beckett had slipped between them again. Quite rightly (though Wally would censure me for saying so).

…where could we find you?

Find me?

At the present moment. If we wanted to get in touch.

Well…I'm here…actually. Sitting in front of you.

(Interview, 2009; p.56)

I think these five lines encapsulate the disease of the age perfectly. N.F. Simpson is now countercultural in a way we could never have anticipated. Wally might have accepted this from *J.C. Mulligan* (2010; p.61–62) as an epitaph, *mutatis mutandis*:

He will be particularly missed by the park bench, the small Jacobean snuff box and the set of brass stair-rods which were his constant companions during his later years.

The 'park bench' points to the life of another, of others, as well as to Mulligan himself. Life, as Simpson sees it, is how he makes us see and we can only benefit from doing so. Enjoy this transcendent writer. Your perspective will never be the same again.

Simon Usher, London, August 2013

(I would like to note Ian Greaves' magnificent work in assembling the text of this book from hundreds of hours of dedicated research. We are hoping it will find its way onto a stage in some form very soon.)

After The Birds

Snippets Two, BBC Radio 3, 16 March 1983. Revised 2006.

It is well known that St Francis preached to the birds, and though one suspects that in many cases it went in one ear and out the other, it was by no means water off a duck's back for the thinking majority. They were the better for it. Indeed, more than one bird became a regular attender at his Sunday morning services as a result of that impromptu sermon. It was while on a visit to North Africa that St Francis found himself addressing a swarm of locusts. To begin with, they were intrigued, but that wore off and soon barely one in three of them was bothering to listen. They had, in any case, as they thought, heard it all before, and it was more fun to go back to poking one another up the backside with their antennae and clambering about on top of one another. And then some electrifying phrase from St Francis would filter through to one of them and, pricking up its ears, it would listen and nudge the others. Soon they would all be listening with rapt attention, determined not to miss a word. The cornfield they were laying waste was forgotten as they hung on his words. So effective, indeed, was the experience, that more than two thirds of the locusts decided for Christ there and then and, mending their ways, never went near a cornfield again, except to test themselves out and see whether, with God's help, they really could resist the temptation to lay it waste. As time went on, they found it increasingly easy and were able to fly off with barely a spasm of the old urge. It was not long before they kicked the habit altogether. It is with some such outcome in mind, that I have tried reading the sermons of St Francis to the greenfly that are plaguing my fuchsias, but, so far, without result.

Always or More

Here is the News, Coventry Theatre, 1960

ALICE
....

STEPHANIE
....

Two elderly but not senile old ladies sit in high-backed armchairs.

ALICE sits upright but not tense and is sewing. She is dressed appropriately and well. She moves very little, and when she does it is with a calculated economy. She is in complete command of herself.

STEPHANIE, smaller, plumper, fussier, wears much the same kind of clothes as ALICE but to quite different effect, since she seems to be at odds with them.

STEPHANIE is completely dominated by ALICE: she has clearly been dominated by her for a very long time: she would indeed find herself at a loss if the dominance were suddenly to disappear. Nevertheless she is constantly drawing for infinitesimal amounts upon a tiny reserve of resistance which never becomes quite exhausted.

A clock with a large face is slightly above head height. By it is a chair with a step, or some other means whereby STEPHANIE can bring her face level with the clock and press against it.

She is standing on this chair tracing the circumference of the clock face with her nose in trying to locate first the hour hand and then the minute hand.

She climbs laboriously down.

ALICE has gone on sewing without reacting in any way.

STEPHANIE: *(As she goes back to her armchair, half to herself, half at large.)* Quarter past nine.

> *ALICE glances briefly and in silence at her wrist watch and without comment goes on sewing. It is a reflex action as much as if the clock itself had chimed instead. This reaction crystallises the relationship between the two women.*

> *STEPHANIE sits silent and fidgetily preoccupied for a few moments.*

STEPHANIE: Alice.

Pause.

ALICE: What is it, Stephanie?

STEPHANIE: My heart, Alice. I think it's stopped beating.

Pause. ALICE without looking up draws in a long, silent breath before answering.

ALICE: *(Behind a façade of patience.)* You know where the stethoscope is, Stephanie.

STEPHANIE gets the stethoscope, puts the end to her heart and proffers the earpieces to ALICE.

ALICE finishes a stitch and looks up for the first time as she takes the earpieces from STEPHANIE in the manner of someone perfunctorily humouring a whim, puts them to her ears and immediately hands them back again.

ALICE: There's nothing wrong with your heart, Stephanie.

In silence, STEPHANIE returns the stethoscope.

Pause.

STEPHANIE: I thought it had stopped beating. *(Making her way back to her armchair.)* I wish I could remember what it was Mr Driver said it had in it. *(Pause.)* Blood, I think he said it was. *(Pause.)* Whatever it was, he said I could rest assured. *(Pause.)* He said if it wasn't that it wouldn't be anything else. *(Pause.)* He did tell me how many ribs I had, too. *(Pause.)* Fourteen, I think he said. But I'm not sure. *(Pause.)* If it was fourteen, I'm one short. *(Pause.)* I wish I could remember. It worries me a little bit. *(Pause.)* I wouldn't worry about my heart so much if I could be sure of my ribs.

ALICE: We're not having you X-rayed at this time of night, Stephanie.

Longer pause. Loud sound of steam escaping.

STEPHANIE: Alice. *(Pause.)* I can hear something. *(Pause.)* I think perhaps I ought to see someone, Alice. *(Pause.)* About hearing things. *(Pause.)* Did you hear anything, Alice?

ALICE: It was Mrs Beglitchen, Stephanie.

Pause. STEPHANIE ponders in surprise.

STEPHANIE: Mrs Beglitchen?

Pause.

ALICE: You've heard Mrs Beglitchen letting off steam before, Stephanie.

STEPHANIE: But not on a Tuesday, Alice.

ALICE: *(Looking directly at STEPHANIE for the first time.)* This is Saturday, Stephanie. *(Reverts to her sewing and speaks again without looking up.)* You get too wrapped up in your own ailments, Stephanie. You're becoming obsessed with them. *(Pause.)* There's a newspaper in the rack. Try and broaden your mind a little bit.

STEPHANIE goes across in a deflated way to the rack, takes out the only newspaper and sits down with it.

She looks at it in silence for a moment or two.

STEPHANIE: I see there's a picture of the Weald of Kent in the paper again, Alice.

Pause.

STEPHANIE throws out the following remarks casually as she lets her eyes wander aimlessly over the paper. Each comment is made with more confidence than the one before it.

STEPHANIE: It's been in there several mornings now. *(Pause.)* Perhaps they can't get it out. *(Pause.)* They had to force it, I expect, when they were getting it in. *(Pause.)* It's wedged itself. *(Pause.)* Perhaps when we get the hot weather it may shrink a little bit. *(Pause.)* And drop out. *(Pause.)* In the heat. Of its own accord. *(Pause.)* I'm surprised one of the cameramen couldn't have got it out. *(Pause.)* Aren't you, Alice? Or the photographer. *(Pause.)* Why don't they crawl underneath, several of them together, and push up? *(Pause.)* While the others are pulling. *(Pause.)* Some of the editors. *(Pause.)* With a hook or something. *(Pause.)* It's disgraceful! Morning after morning!

Pause.

ALICE: It's two years now since that paper was delivered, Stephanie.

STEPHANIE looks at the date at the top of the paper. Her confidence suddenly evaporates.

ALICE: We have this every day.

STEPHANIE: This is the one that was on the table this morning, Alice. When I came down. It wasn't in the rack.

ALICE looks pointedly at STEPHANIE.

STEPHANIE: I found it over there on the table by the door.

ALICE: That's where it always is first thing in the morning, Stephanie. You should know that by now. I told you when I stopped the paper that you'd have to get used to the same one for a little while. You should try and make it last.

Long pause. STEPHANIE, desperately trying not to go under, returns the paper to the rack.

ALICE: *(Without looking up.)* Under the china cabinet.

STEPHANIE goes there, takes out a tin helmet, puts it on, and continues looking about the room.

ALICE: *(After a brief pause.)* Over there. By the door.

STEPHANIE goes to the door and takes up a sten gun.

ALICE: *(Behind a façade of concern.)* There are soldiers for all this Stephanie.

STEPHANIE goes silently out.

ALICE: *(Calling after her.)* If it rains during the night, remember you've got your groundsheet. Make yourself a bivouac.

ALICE does a few more stitches and then puts down her sewing.

She gets up, takes the newspaper out of the rack, carefully re-folds it, smoothing out the creases and making it neat and presentable, and puts it very deliberately on the table near the door.

She puts out the light and goes up to bed.

Fade.

Compilation One: Anatomy of Bewilderment, 2009. Previously unpublished.

Anyone's Gums Can Listen to Reason

Play Ten (Edward Arnold, 1977)

STEVE	TWENTIES
HARRIET	TWENTIES
FRANCES	TWENTIES
MR BRILL	FIFTIES
MRS PERCEVAL	FIFTIES
MR CANTILEVER	FIFTIES

Simple Quaker Meeting Hall. Three or four rows of wooden benches set like pews across the stage so that the congregation is facing downstage. The congregation consists of STEVE, HARRIET and FRANCES only, although there is room for perhaps thirty people. They are spaced out over the room. They sit silent and natural and relaxed as the lights go up, their minds open to whatever the spirit may move one or other of them to say. For some moments there is silence, and then, without rising, HARRIET speaks in a soft, unemphatic voice as though reading a story.

HARRIET: There was a sound like small marbles dropping on to the floor…some twenty or thirty of them…and Mr Murgatroyd, clearly troubled at what he suspected might be the cause, stepped back from the painting at which he had been gazing with such intensity until that moment, and looked down and around him in consternation. As he turned, I could see that his lips were drawn in over his gums, as might be those of someone who had just lost all his teeth. Mrs Pertwee, who had heard the sound too, looked at the floor and at once got the message. 'Oh, no!' she cried.

HARRIET falls silent. After a moment, STEVE stands and speaks.

STEVE: 'What is it?' shouted Kate from the kitchen.

STEVE sits. After a moment, FRANCES speaks without rising.

FRANCES: 'It's nothing,' called back Lily, who was also in the room. 'All Mr Murgatroyd's teeth have dropped out, that's all.'

MR BRILL quietly enters and sits by himself.

HARRIET: This was indeed what had happened. His gums, for the second time that week, had gone on strike.

STEVE: 'It's no good trying to put them back in,' said Mr Murgatroyd, as people began to hand his teeth one by one back to him. 'Not while my gums are in this mood.'

HARRIET: 'Surely they can be talked to,' said Father O'Flaherty, who had just come into the room.

FRANCES: 'Talked to?' said Mr Murgatroyd, with a hollow laugh. 'You must be joking!'

STEVE: 'But *anyone's* gums can listen to reason!' expostulated Edith, who until that moment had been lying behind the sofa, fast asleep.

MRS PERCIVAL enters on the next line, and sits, also by herself.

FRANCES: 'Like hell they can!' said Canon Copley, entering the room, and speaking forthrightly as ever.

HARRIET: 'Gums are eminently amenable to reason,' returned Edith, sticking to her guns. 'They're known for it.'

MR CANTILEVER has followed hard on the heels of MRS PERCEVAL and unobtrusively finds a place by himself to sit.

STEVE: 'You don't know *my* gums,' said Mr Murgatroyd, ruefully.

HARRIET: 'This isn't the first time, you see,' said Lily, chipping in. 'It's happened before.'

FRANCES: 'You should read the Riot Act to them,' said Kate, still fuming. 'All they want is a skive. Put their feet up and have a smoke. Under cover of industrial action. They'd get a piece of my mind if they were my gums!' she said.

There is a silence for some moments. When the three older people begin to speak, they do so like people striking up a conversation in, say, a bus queue. The only difference is that they speak without actually addressing one another. They are expressing what is in their own minds rather than, as in the case of the younger people, seeming to pick it up out of the atmosphere.

CANTILEVER: No hardship for them to stir themselves. Hold a few teeth in position once in a while. It's after all what they're there for.

PERCEVAL: They could at least make a show of earning their keep.

BRILL: They've got precious little else to do.

CANTILEVER: Mine certainly haven't.

PERCEVAL: If they're not doing that, they're kicking their heels and getting bored and making a nuisance of themselves.

BRILL: Or sitting with their feet up.

During what follows, and while the three younger people sit quietly in a state of meditative calm, tuned in to eternity, the three older people gradually start to talk to one another, so that, although they do not change their positions, there is an interplay between them as of people exchanging views in a waiting room and finding themselves in broad agreement.

PERCEVAL: There's no gainsaying that a man whose gums are pulling their weight is in a far happier position than one whose teeth are allowed to do as they like because his gums don't care.

BRILL: Firmly anchored teeth are in the main contented teeth.

CANTILEVER: Teeth which, come mealtime, will buckle down and get on with the job.

BRILL: With a smile on their lips.

CANTILEVER: A smile on their lips and a song in their hearts.

PERCEVAL: And not just one tooth at a time.

BRILL: Team spirit.

PERCEVAL: All the teeth working harmoniously together – hand in glove – for the good of the whole organism.

CANTILEVER: And in partnership with the jaws.

BRILL: In partnership with the jaws to get the food not only chewed but effectively chewed.

Pause.

CANTILEVER: Unhappy the man whose upper right molar doesn't know what his lower left canine is doing.

BRILL: A failure in communication.

CANTILEVER: Whereby some of the food gets chewed seven or eight times over whilst other food is not chewed at all.

BRILL: And this makes for bad feeling.

PERCEVAL: Particularly in the case of food that feels itself neglected but doesn't like to come forward for fear of being thought to be fussing or drawing attention to itself unnecessarily.

Long pause.

CANTILEVER: Who was it encountered one of his front teeth at Waterloo Station with a pair of binoculars slung round its shoulders?

BRILL: Haydn.

CANTILEVER: 'Where you off to?'

PERCEVAL: 'Ascot.'

BRILL: They please themselves.

CANTILEVER: No amount of remonstrance…

BRILL: Oh, no. Couldn't care less.

PERCEVAL: I think probably that Galileo had more trouble with his teeth than almost anyone.

BRILL: Particularly his wisdom teeth.

CANTILEVER: Which were invariably in the public library whenever he wanted to chew with them.

BRILL: And no change, either, from his incisors.

PERCEVAL: His incisors were as likely as not wandering hand-in-hand through some meadow or other picking daisies.

CANTILEVER: When they weren't down on the beach watching the tide come in and go out.

BRILL: One might just as well not have any teeth.

CANTILEVER: They can lead you a right old dance if you don't watch them.

PERCEVAL: Not that I've any complaint against mine, touch wood. They pull their weight reasonably well.

BRILL: Mine, I must say, do a perfectly good job.

PERCEVAL: They're not all tarred with the same brush.

BRILL: The last time mine had any sort of break was in 1954. When they went to see Marlon Brando in *On the Waterfront*. They sat in the two and threes. As it was then.

PERCEVAL: Did they enjoy it?

BRILL: They liked bits of it. They weren't, as I remember, any too smitten with the way it was done, but Brando they thought superb.

CANTILEVER: Old Mrs Frobisher's teeth were into films quite a lot.

BRILL: Mrs Frobisher's teeth were into everything.

PERCEVAL: They led a pretty lively existence.

CANTILEVER: Precious little time for Mrs Frobisher in the end, if the truth were told.

BRILL: She had them out eventually. To hell with it.

PERCEVAL: You can hardly blame her.

CANTILEVER: It's coming to something, when your own teeth not only go to the pictures without so much as a by-your-leave, but choose whereabouts they're going to sit in that lordly manner, and generally carry on as if they were a law unto themselves.

BRILL: I can't imagine anybody in his right mind and with an atom of self-respect allowing himself to be dictated to in matters of that kind by his teeth.

PERCEVAL: He might consult them.

BRILL: He might consult them, largely out of politeness and to let them feel that they're being kept in the picture, but he wouldn't necessarily feel himself bound.

CANTILEVER: A man kow-towing to his own teeth…it would be a pretty unedifying spectacle. It's a pusillanimous stance to adopt.

PERCEVAL: There's no denying a lot of people do, for better or worse, allow their teeth a fair measure of independence.

BRILL: No one's advocating an unduly authoritarian attitude, but – aesthetic considerations apart and regardless of whether they're qualified or not – to let your teeth make decisions of that nature is to let the tail wag the dog on a pretty gargantuan scale.

CANTILEVER: Upper and lower set marching straight to the most expensive seats with their owner trailing ignominiously along behind them is hardly a very uplifting sight.

BRILL: Show me a man who allows himself to be overborne by his teeth, and I'll show you a man who's in deep trouble.

CANTILEVER: A sad day for the cinema when that sort of consideration determines what we see on our screens. The cultural life of the country would have to be at a pretty low ebb.

The three older people relapse into silence.

STEVE: All Mr Murgatroyd's teeth were by this time gathered up and handed back.

HARRIET: 'What are you going to do with them?' asked Mrs Pertwee, ever practical.

FRANCES: 'I've got a matchbox,' he said. 'They can go in there.'

Pause.

HARRIET: But, search as he would through all his pockets, no matchbox could be found.

STEVE: It was the work, however, of a moment to drop the teeth into his pocket.

FRANCES: Where they remained.

Pause.

STEVE: After a little while, the teeth were beginning to burn a hole in his pocket and he got up and went to the mirror. 'I'm wondering,' he said, 'whether it's safe to put them back in.' 'There's no harm in trying,' said Lily. 'If it weren't for my gums being bolshie, I wouldn't hesitate,' he said.

FRANCES: 'They want a good belt up the backside,' said Mrs Pertwee, speaking for them all.

HARRIET: 'They'll get it one of these days,' said Mr Murgatroyd, slipping his teeth back in one at a time.

FRANCES: 'Fingers crossed,' said Mrs Grover.

STEVE: 'Heaven be praised,' said Mr Murgatroyd, 'they're all back and, so far – touch wood – they're staying put.'

HARRIET: 'Oh, yes,' said Kate, appearing at the door, 'you look a treat with your teeth in.'

FRANCES: 'He certainly does,' said Canon Copley, and the others concurred.

HARRIET: 'Now perhaps I can go out and face my public,' he said, going out.

Pause.

HARRIET: 'What a fuss,' said Lily, 'about a few teeth!'

FRANCES: 'Fuss indeed,' said the others, with warmth.

Pause.

Slow fade.

introducing leisure promotions

leisure promotions

leisure promotions has come into being in the belief that many discriminating people demand more from life than the privilege of looking on at it, and that for such people violence, crime, disease and vice cannot be savoured and enjoyed to the full through the medium of newspapers and television alone. The needs of a healthily morbid imagination can be met, however, only by a degree of personal involvement such as few of us have the time or the means to bring about by ourselves: street accidents do not after all happen outside our own front door every day of the week - nor is it always easy or convenient to engineer them; most of us are debarred from entering the operating theatre; and it is rarely our own or our neighbours' womenfolk who are molested on their way home from work. So perhaps it is not surprising that more and more people should be turning to **leisure promotions** which

by virtue of vast resources such as only a large organisation can afford to maintain, is able to offer a range of firsthand experiences far beyond the reach of the ordinary private connoisseur.

TO THOSE WHO ASPIRE TO THE FULLY
LIVED LIFE **leisure promotions**

BRINGS THE DIRECTLY EXPERIENCED
EXPERIENCE."

If you would like to be put in touch with life at its most nauseating, vicious, gruesome and sadistic - a card or a phone call to **leisure promotions**

is all that is necessary. The cost is very modest indeed. Why not put an end to frustration once and for all by contacting us NOW ?

(A DREDGEKIND & GRODMARK ADVERTISEMENT)

DIRECTOR
MANAGING DIRECTOR
MANAGER
COPYWRITER
LAYOUT MAN
MAINTENANCE ENGINEER
TYPIST
NIGHTWATCHMAN

N.F.SIMPSON

Mr. Dredgekind and
Mr. Grodmark.

Can You Hear Me?

One to Another, Lyric Hammersmith, 1959

HUD
....
CROB
....
VOICE
....
VOICE 1
....
VOICE 2
....

A hotel room.

When the lights come up HUD sits reading a paper. CROB is moving restlessly about.

CROB: You don't happen to know where there's a speaking tube?

HUD: *(Looking up.)* What?

CROB: I want to put my ear to a speaking tube.

HUD: *(Reverting to the paper.)* They'll send you one up if you ring down.

CROB: I just feel like it. Where's the phone?

HUD: *(Without looking up.)* You used it last.

CROB: And I put it back. *(Looking for the telephone.)* I put it back over there by the window.

HUD: I haven't touched it.

CROB: Somebody has, for God's sake. It isn't there now.

HUD: It'll turn up.

CROB: *(Abandoning the search.)* There's probably a speaking tube somewhere if I knew where to look for it.

HUD: *(Looking up.)* A what?

CROB: A speaking tube. It isn't often I feel like this.

HUD: Like what?

CROB: I just happen to be in the mood. Something controversial. Or a man reading bits from *Lorna Doone* as far as that goes. As long as it's something you can listen to.

You'd think they'd have a speaking tube, wouldn't you, in a room this size?

HUD: *(Folding paper.)* I can lend you an ear trumpet if you want to shout down that?

CROB: I don't want to shout down anything. I want to listen.

HUD: In that case there isn't very much I can do for you.

CROB: What are we paying for this room? Something bloody astronomic, and they can't even supply speaking tubes.

HUD: Not much demand is there? Most people want ear trumpets.

CROB: I thought this was the sort of place where they're supposed to cater for everybody.

HUD: You can't expect them to put a speaking tube in every single room in the building just in case somebody might take it into his head to put his ear to one. Be reasonable.

There is a brief pause.

HUD: What's wrong with shouting down an ear trumpet –

CROB: God help me!

HUD: – like anybody else?

CROB: I wonder if there's a speaking tube in the bedroom?

CROB goes off.

HUD: There might be. Why don't you forget about it and come out?

CROB: *(Off.)* Where to?

HUD: Just over the way. There'll only be a few of us.

Pause.

HUD: We usually get together once or twice a week.

Pause.

HUD: What about it?

CROB: *(Off.)* What are you going to *do*, for God's sake?

HUD: We just take our ear trumpets along. Eight or nine of us.

CROB: *(Off.)* A shouting party, eh?

HUD: It'll take you out of yourself.

CROB: *(Off.)* No, thanks.

HUD: You don't have to worry about an ear trumpet – you can take mine.

CROB enters.

HUD: I've got a spare one.

CROB: I'd sooner stay where I am, thanks very much. If I knew where I could put my hand on a speaking tube.

HUD: You won't find one in here. *(He goes towards the door.)*

CROB: If you're going down by the lift you might ask them to send me one up.

HUD: *(At the door.)* About time you got out. Sitting huddled up there over a speaking tube.

CROB: Have a good shout, won't you?

HUD: *(Closing the door.)* I always do.

HUD exits. CROB hesitates for a moment and then begins restlessly looking round again. There is a knock at the door.

CROB: Yes? *(He goes to the door and opens it. There is no one there. He shrugs and closes the door. He continues casting around for places where he might find a speaking tube.)*

There is a knock at the door. CROB looks in exasperation towards the door and crosses to it. He opens the door.

VOICE: *(Off.)* With the compliments of the manager, sir.

CROB takes a speaking tube.

VOICE: *(Off.)* I knocked a moment ago but there was no one here.

CROB: So I noticed. Shouldn't there be one of these in the room.

VOICE: *(Off.)* They were taken out during the bombing, sir.

CROB: It's a bit much if I have to send down for one every time, isn't it?

VOICE: *(Off.)* I'll make enquiries, sir.

CROB: What about?

VOICE: *(Off.)* Sir?

CROB: Never mind. What do I do with this?

VOICE: *(Off.)* You put your ear to it, sir.

CROB does so. He listens. His face expresses interest and amusement. He chuckles.

CROB: *(To the boy at the door.)* Right. This'll do. *(He continues to listen. He glances up and realizing the boy is still there, impatiently takes out a coin and hands it to the boy and without taking his ear from the speaking tube tries to close the door.)*

VOICE: *(Off.)* Thank you, sir.

The length of tube prevents CROB from closing the door, which he leaves ajar, drawing the tube into the room after him. He listens for a moment with all the rapture of an addict and then, turning off the sound near the nozzle, finds a means of supporting the tube so that the nozzle hangs down just above head height. To this he fixes a large spray. He turns on the sound to test it.

A man's voice is heard.

VOICE 1: *(Very loud.)* You mustn't expect too much, Mrs Beltlock.

CROB, scalded, hurriedly turns off the sound, adjusts it, and turns it on again.

Two men's voices are heard. The volume is normal and the tone reasonable.

VOICE 1: Yes. Well, we'll do what we can for you, Mrs Beltlock. But don't expect miracles.

VOICE 2: Croft. Bullingham Croft.

VOICE 1: Yes. Well, as I say, Mr Croft, it's no use expecting miracles, but we'll do everything we can.

CROB has made minor adjustments and now, satisfied, turns off the sound. He takes off his shirt and prepares to wash himself under the spray.

As he turns it on the same two voices are heard.

VOICE 2: If you could just get it working at half-cock, it would be something.

VOICE 1: Three-quarters cock if it can possibly be managed, Mrs Croft.

VOICE 2: Beltlock.

VOICE 1: Mr Beltlock. Leave it with us, and when we're finished you can get in touch with us.

VOICE 2: Thank you very much.

VOICE 1: Just give us a ring.

VOICE 2: I'll try and get hold of your phone number.

VOICE 1: Let us know how you get on.

VOICE 2: I will.

VOICE 1: Good-bye and good luck.

> *CROB has finished washing. He turns off the sound and quickly rubs himself with a towel, goes off into the bedroom and returns with a sun-ray lamp. He detaches the speaking tube from the spray and fixes it to the sun-ray lamp. He puts on dark glasses, takes out sun-tan lotion and switches on. As the words come out he makes himself comfortable and sits rubbing himself with the lotion. The VOICE speaks very rapidly.*

VOICE 2: If you can find an old overcoat at home I suggest you stand it up in a corner. You can read the Gettysburg speech to it from time to time. It won't do any good, of course – but it won't do any harm. Or if you can't stand it up, put it on. I should button it up well if you do that and anchor it down. And why not give it a coat of paint at the same time? Make it ship-shape. Go round it with an oil-can. That's what I usually do. Then I just run it up and down an inclined plane two or three times and put it back in the cupboard. It keeps them in good trim. I've had mine now since I was ten and it's still going like a bird. It belonged to my uncle originally, so you can imagine it's pretty old. One of the things I really shall have to do one of these days is go through the lining. See where it brings me out. I've never been. I could probably do it in ten minutes on a bike, but somehow I never seem to get round to it. And you never know who you're going to meet on the way. Might keep you talking for an hour or more. You know how it is. Hallo – what's this? *(Intensely.)* Specks? And some more on the sleeve here. What are *they* doing? And all down the back. This has been left out overnight. In the rain. It's got rust all over it.

As the voice becomes more intense CROB moves gradually back as though the heat were becoming uncomfortable.

VOICE 2: Unless it's woodworm. God help us if it's woodworm. Yes. That's what it *is*. These are holes. I thought they were specks of rust but they're holes. It's riddled with them. I wish I'd noticed this before. If that's woodworm in there I don't know what we can do. Why didn't I spot this weeks ago? Once they've had time to get right inside it's the devil's own job to coax the little beggers out again. Barney! Ralph! Sam! You see? We're hamstrung. We don't even know their names.

VOICE 1: Perhaps if we rang a bell?

VOICE 2: No. Once this happens you just have to go in after them. You stay there. See that no one comes in. If I'm not back in half an hour you know what to do.

VOICE 1: Careful, Chief. They may be armed.

VOICE 2: *(Echoing.)* Sure I'll be careful.

HUD enters. He has an ear trumpet which he puts down. He takes out a throat lozenge and puts it in his mouth.

HUD: *(Very hoarsely.)* Boy, am I hoarse?

There is a roar of detonation from the sun-ray lamp. CROB gives a cry of pain and leaps up. HUD wrenches out the plug. Silence.

VOICE 2: *(Very hoarsely.)* Why can't you shout down an ear trumpet like anybody else?

HUD coughs violently.

Black out.

N. F. SIMPSON

Canoe Salesman

The Dick Emery Show, BBC One, 19 January 1980

MR FULHAM

GILBERT PROTHEROE

WOMAN

A wooden house high in the mountains.

Door knock. MR FULHAM emerges via staircase and crosses room to answer it. PROTHEROE is at the door.

PROTHEROE: Mr Fulham?

FULHAM: Yes.

PROTHEROE: *(Announcing himself.)* Gilbert Protheroe.

FULHAM: Gilbert who?

PROTHEROE: Gilbert Protheroe. I'm here to sell you a collapsible canvas canoe.

FULHAM: I beg your pardon?

PROTHEROE: *(Inviting himself in.)* Tidal waves…floods… cloudbursts…anything in that nature. You'll be sitting pretty if you happen to possess a collapsible canvas canoe. In fact you'd have the decided edge on those who would otherwise be called upon to drown! *(Laughs to himself.)*

FULHAM: Yes, I'm sure. It sounds like a tempting proposition but we are a bit above sea level here for that sort of thing. I mean, at this altitude you'd have to have the water sent up if you wanted something to float a canoe on.

PROTHEROE: I see…yes, it's funny you should say that. Have a look at this. *(Produces a small stone.)*

FULHAM: What is it?

PROTHEROE: *(Despairingly.)* It's a stone. I found it outside your door as I came in. Now, if you look very closely you'll see there's an imprint of a fossil on it, a species of fish.

FULHAM: *(Interested.)* Oh so there is, yes.

PROTHEROE: Now I reckon you and I would have had to have lived…ooh, several hundred thousand million years ago to have met that fish in the flesh, Mr Fulham. It's now extinct.

FULHAM: Good Lord.

PROTHEROE: Which proves conclusively that you are residing on what, several thousand million years ago, was nothing less than the ocean bed.

FULHAM: The ocean bed?

PROTHEROE: Yes. *(With an air of triumph.)* And what was once the ocean bed could very well be the ocean bed again! It only requires a geographical cataclysm of global proportions and you could be under fifty thousand fathoms of salt water without even realising it.

FULHAM: Crikey!

PROTHEROE: Crikey indeed! And in my book, Mr Fulham, nobody but a madman would want to be caught napping when it happened. I mean, after all, they jeered Noah, but who had the last laugh there?

FULHAM: Yes, but that was a good few thousand years ago.

PROTHEROE: Precisely. And never another catastrophe on anything like the same scale since. Now I ask you, it can't last forever. I mean, you'd be living in a fool's paradise if you thought that was any safeguard.

FULHAM: Oh would I?

PROTHEROE: Oh yes indeed. I mean, you're sitting on a volcano if you did but know it.

FULHAM: *(Rushing to window in concern.)* Good grief! *(Quickly returns.)* Tell me, I mean – please, what is the answer?

PROTHEROE: *(Produces an ordinary handkerchief, unfolds and holds it up with fingers pinching top corners.)* This.

FULHAM: That?

PROTHEROE: Absolutely.

FULHAM: Yes, but that wouldn't keep me afloat for very long.

PROTHEROE: No, granted, but you've got another seven hundred and fifty of these still to come.

FULHAM: *(Enthused.)* Ah, now you're talking!

PROTHEROE: Sewn together, waterproofed and stretched over a specially constructed canoe-shaped wooden frame…and you'll have a purpose built, ocean-going craft second to none.

FULHAM: I see. *(Points at handkerchief as PROTHEROE folds it up.)* That being…

PROTHEROE: The first basic unit, which for a down payment of only ten pounds is yours entirely free of charge.

FULHAM: Well that sounds very reasonable.

PROTHEROE: *(Considers.)* Of course, bought outright the whole canoe could cost you somewhere well in the region of two thousand pounds, but for a payment of only ten pounds monthly for each of the seven hundred and fifty-one units, you could build a canoe over the years without putting any strain on your budget at any one time.

FULHAM: Well I must say that sounds excellent value for money!

PROTHEROE: Ha ha, does it? Oh yes, of course it does! And what's more it's not the sort of service we can afford to give to anyone.

FULHAM: You mean to say I have been specially singled out?

PROTHEROE: Oh yes, we saw you coming… I mean, or rather, you were the coming man when it came to handing out the key positions after the Holocaust and therefore someone to be given first priority as the most vital person to be saved.

FULHAM: *(Flattered.)* Really?!

PROTHEROE: Yes!

FULHAM: *(Getting up, producing cheque book and pen.)* Well, tell me, who do I make out the cheque to?

PROTHEROE: Gilbert Protheroe, Collapsible Canvas Canoe Company.

FULHAM: *(Begins.)* G. Protheroe… *(Halts.)* Now just a minute. What happens in the event of the flood occurring before…

PROTHEROE: The canoe is completed? Ah well, in that case Mr Fulham you don't have to pay a penny piece more, ever.

FULHAM: Good God!

PROTHEROE: Yes. Now in the case of one of our dearer models, that represents quite a considerable saving.

FULHAM: Really?

PROTHEROE: Oh yes. And in fact, if the water were to rise at all rapidly you'd save more in the matter of minutes by simply drowning than anyone could earn in a lifetime.

FULHAM: Ah! *(Returns to writing cheque.)*

PROTHEROE: The same applies if you were blown up or even buried under an avalanche for some reason.

FULHAM: *(Tearing cheque out, contemplates.)* What if someone were to stick a knife in my back?

PROTHEROE: Oh, exactly the same applies. Anything involving sudden decease and your payments end automatically.

FULHAM: Well I must say that's an exceedingly generous concession!

PROTHEROE: *(Accepting cheque.)* Well we try to help people Mr Fulham.

FULHAM: In fact, looking at it from a worldly wise point of view the answer would seem to be to opt for the most expensive model you have and then pray for a quick death.

PROTHEROE: Yes, well that way you'd certainly make a killing. *(Breaking.)* Well, it's been a pleasure to do business with you Mr Fulham. *(They shake hands.)* Thank you very much indeed. *(FULHAM gestures.)* Oh, I'm so sorry! *(Produces handkerchief, which he hands to FULHAM.)* Thank you very much.

FULHAM: Thank you!

(They head to door.)

PROTHEROE: Ha ha, cheers.

PROTHEROE exits.

Exterior. A WOMAN stands waiting as PROTHEROE appears.

PROTHEROE: *(Taking WOMAN's arm.)* We'll use your Cami Knicks next time, darling! *(Beaming at cheque.)* Let's get down the bank with this before it closes!

Interior.

FULHAM anxiously taps hanging barometer and darts to the window, clutching handkerchief for dear life.

The Chinese Box

Punch, 1 December 1965

MR LONGSTOP, Minister for Foreign Relations (Kettlemarket, Labour)

MR J.T. BOWLER (Leatherbridge South, Labour)

MR BOUMINSTER-GULLY (Ambleport East, Conservative)

SIR ENOCH BATSMAN (Bournecaster, Labour)

MR REGINALD SCORER (Darlingside North, Conservative)

MR L.P. COVER (Southbaston, Labour)

The speaker took the chair at half past two o'clock.

BOWLER asked the Minister for Foreign Relations whether any request had been made by a private firm of cardboard-box manufacturers for permission to present Mao Tse-tung with one of its products as a gesture of goodwill from this country to the People's Republic of China on the occasion of his forthcoming state visit to this country; and if so, what reply had been given.

LONGSTOP: As honourable members will no doubt be aware, China is a somewhat large country. *(Laughter.)* It is a country which has long been burdened, through a geographical accident which is no fault of its own, with a great deal more space than it can conveniently find room for. The government, therefore, is disposed to give favourable consideration to a suggestion by The New Era Box Manufacturing Company that a gift to the head of such a country might suitably take the form of an empty cardboard box, in which a little of this space could be stored away. Such a gift, it is felt, could make a very real contribution towards the lessening of tensions between East and West.

BOWLER: May we know from the Minister whether any kind of wish has been expressed by Mao Tse-tung for a cardboard box from The New Era Box Manufacturing Company?

LONGSTOP: To the best of my knowledge no approach of any kind has been made by Mao Tse-tung or any other head of state with a view to acquiring a cardboard box from this country. The initiative has been entirely with The New Era Box Manufacturing Company itself. Indeed, I should have thought it to be in the nature of a gesture of this kind that it should be both spontaneous and unexpected. *(Cheers.)*

BOUMINSTER-GULLY: Is the Minister entirely convinced that it is in the national interest to make presents to the heads of countries whose intentions towards us may or may not be friendly, of large cardboard boxes which could in all probability later be used against us?

LONGSTOP: In referring to 'large cardboard boxes,' the honourable member is, if I may say so, jumping the gun. No decision as to the size of the box has yet been arrived at. Discussions about it are still going on. As for its later being used against us, this is a contingency so remote as to be discounted.

BATSMAN: Can the Minister assure the House that due consideration will in fact be given to the question of size, bearing in mind not only the use to which the box is to be put, but the fact that it is to be presented to a man who is – whether we like it or not – the leader of some six hundred and fifty million people? The size ought surely to bear some relation to the importance and standing of the recipient. Perhaps there are precedents by which the Government could be guided in this matter?

LONGSTOP: No precedent, unfortunately, exists in this instance, and it is for this reason all the more necessary, as honourable members will readily appreciate, that we should act with the utmost tact and discretion. The New Era Box Manufacturing Company is itself aware of the extreme delicacy of the situation, and has in fact expressed a wish to co-operate fully with the government in this matter should the proposal be fully accepted. The crux of the difficulty lies in the fact that a box of adequate cubic capacity, bearing in mind the status of the recipient, would have to cover an area roughly equivalent to Regent's Park and be two miles high. In the view of the government, a box constructed on this scale might well prove an embarrassment to the recipient and so defeat its own purpose.

SCORER: Can those of us who have doubts about the wisdom of this whole venture be given an assurance that what is intended as a bona fide gesture of goodwill will not be allowed to degenerate into a piece of plain, old-fashioned appeasement? *(Some opposition cheers.)*

LONGSTOP: There is a very clear distinction between a gesture of goodwill and an act of appeasement, and the government is fully aware of the need to see that this distinction does not become in any way blurred. *(Government cheers.)*

SCORER: Will the Minister enlarge a little on the actual measures he envisages to ensure this?

LONGSTOP: Honourable members may rest assured that we shall be watching Mao Tse-tung's reaction very closely at the time the presentation of the box is made, and that any abatement of hostility seen to be occasioned by it will be subjected to the closest possible scrutiny. It may well be that as a result of this we shall find it necessary to offset the effect of the gift by some action of a less friendly nature. In this connection several possibilities are under consideration, including the pulling away of his chair as he is about to sit down in it. The situation, however, is complicated by the equally paramount need to avoid going too far in the other direction and actually intensifying his hostility. This might well take us over the edge into deliberate provocation. We must aim to strike as exact a balance as possible, if we are to avoid the charge on the one hand of appeasement and on the other of provocation. The most practicable solution would seem to be some kind of body blow, delivered to the solar plexus at the same time as the gift is made, and with such force as is appropriate having in mind the size of the box. The two will then, it is hoped, cancel each other out.

BATSMAN: In view of the extreme difficulty of judging with any exactitude the force of the blow within such fine limits as would be required, does the Minister not think that the blow should be delivered first, and the size of the box determined subsequently from this?

LONGSTOP: Such a possibility is one of a number which are before the government, but the principle which has been adopted is that the force of the blow should be determined by the size of the box, and not vice versa.

COVER: Can the Minister tell us what is to be done about the space inside the box? Is this also to go to Mao Tse-tung? And if so, is it not a thoroughly irresponsible action on the part of the government to allow this to happen in view of the permanent state of overcrowding which exists in these islands?

LONGSTOP: The space inside the box will of course remain the property of Her Majesty's government, and is not intended to form any part of the gift to Mao Tse-tung, which is of a cardboard box only. The onus of providing the space with which to fill it will be upon Mao Tse-tung himself. I cannot say that I envisage his encountering any insuperable difficulty here. China, as I have already pointed out to honourable members, is a large country.

BATSMAN: Would the minister not agree that, notwithstanding the somewhat carping spirit in which certain honourable members have received this very generous proposal, The New Era Box Manufacturing Company is to be congratulated on its public-spirited action? *(Some government and opposition cheers.)*

LONGSTOP: I for one would be happy to associate myself with such a sentiment. As I have repeatedly made clear, this is an issue – whatever decision about it we may finally arrive at – which has no political significance whatever. It is simply and solely a gesture of goodwill made by private enterprise on its own initiative and on behalf of us all as a contribution towards the easing of tension between East and West. *(Cheers.)* As such, I think it is heartily to be applauded. *(Cheers.)* We on our side will have done our part. The rest will be up to Mao Tse-tung.

Cross Examination

Compilation One: Anatomy of Bewilderment, 2009.
Previously unpublished.

Let me take you back a number of years to the time when as a young man of twenty or so you were bitten by the bug of ventriloquism. It would not be too much to say that you were something of an enthusiast, were you not?

I dabbled.

You did indeed dabble. To the extent of practising your ventriloquism at weekends on, I believe, Clapham Common.

I was experimenting.

Trying to throw your voice further and further, no doubt.

Yes.

Further on one occasion, I would suggest, than you'd intended, since it ended up in Bognor.

Who in his right mind would want to throw his voice to a place like Bognor?

I believe it was unintentional, my lord.

Curious predilection. Carry on.

You have begun in recent years, albeit in a more clandestine manner, to take up ventriloquism again, retiring behind closed doors in order to try once more to throw your voice – this time simply from one end of the room to the other.

Only once.

This was an upstairs room, was it not?

It was on the first floor.

An upstairs room with casement windows, one of which was wide open.

I forgot to close it.

Your voice, as I think all of us here in Court have had ample reason to observe, is a fairly powerful one. And what I am suggesting to you now is that, as you struggled to throw your voice across the room, you began little by little to find your considerably more powerful voice slowly but surely getting the upper hand. Eventually, grapple with it as you might, your voice got the better of you and the tables were dramatically turned when your voice, having succeeded finally in overpowering you, threw you bodily from one side of the room to the other, as a result of which you went sailing out through the open window, landing rather heavily on the ground outside, whence, having picked yourself up, you returned to recover your voice from the room where, doubtless with a smirk on its face, it was awaiting you.

I landed in a flowerbed.

A flowerbed in which was a number of substantial rocks.

I was building a rockery.

Your injuries in short were sustained in a manner totally at variance with the one you described to us so graphically earlier.

Some of them might have been.

Thank you.

&DG

leisure promotions

N. F. Simpson

N. F. SIMPSON

DIRECTOR
MANAGING DIRECTOR
MANAGER
COPYWRITER
LAYOUT MAN
MAINTENANCE ENGINEER
TYPIST
NIGHTWATCHMAN

A NEW
WAY TO IMPRESS
YOUR
FRIENDS :!

BE PHOTOGRAPHED
ASSAULTING A SEX-
MANIAC !

---

leisure promotions

FIRST
FIRST NOW

to bring Crime to you in your own HOME !

to put you in the forefront of the Fight AGAINST Crime !

● ARREST a member of the Criminal Classes (handcuffs provided)

● OUTWIT a clever and resourceful crook with the aid of experienced detectives

● SOLVE a baffling crime by a special NEW foolproof method

● TAKE PART in a nation-wide manhunt

Write NOW for details

(A DREDGEKIND & GRODMARK ADVERTISEMENT)

The Crozier

Compilation One: Anatomy of Bewilderment, 2009.
Previously unpublished.

Thoughtful piece in *The Times* today about the state of the church. Religion in the doldrums and we cast wildly about for an explanation. Daphne (Gudgeon) looks in on her way to the Post Office. 'I blame one thing and one thing alone, Christopher. The crozier.' Am inclined to agree. 'That thing has been a thoroughly pernicious influence from the moment it was introduced.' Would hardly go so far as this, but am reminded by it of the notorious prelate whose name escapes me but who is said to have made it his practice to give people what he called 'a crafty poke up the backside' with a crozier specially designed for the purpose, if so be that it seemed an appropriate moment for winning them over to the faith by unorthodox means. Raise the matter with Basil and Thelma over dinner. (One listens with a certain amount of respect to what they have to say on the matter of croziers in that a second cousin by marriage of Thelma's daily help had a great-great-grandfather – a shepherd in, I believe, Aberdeen – whose second cousin by marriage once possessed a replica of an ancient shepherd's crook, which he kept on the wall above the mantelpiece in his sitting room.) They take the line that, yes, admittedly one has all too often seen the crozier abused, but that there have been times nevertheless when the crozier has come quite magnificently into its own, proving its worth beyond any real possibility of argument. Basil cites the case, referred to in Baxter's *Ecclesiastical Furniture*, of 'the bishop who, emulating the action of a pole-vaulter in the privacy of his own grounds, arrives unbidden and by inadvertence in next door's garden's rainwater-butt head first. It is, nine times out of ten, only his crozier, protruding from the surface of the water like a periscope, that proclaims his presence there.' I counter with the case of St Boniface the Twenty-third, who on one occasion went out leaving his crozier leaning against the hatstand only, on coming back, to notice that it was slightly bent. On instituting enquiries, it came to light that his son-in-law had been using it to prise open the door of his chicken hut. An abuse of the crozier? Not so in Thelma's view. (True that such practices, *if carried too far*, could be said to do little by way of enhancing the reputation of the Church, but it was for this reason that at the Synod of Whitby firm guidelines were quite properly drawn up.) Daphne, when we next meet, pooh-poohs all this. What, she says, and I suppose it's a good point, of the cleric who runs a small grocery business in, as it may be, Carshalton, on the side and, a crozier happening to have been left behind by some absentminded visiting bishop, he decides to make use of it for hooking down packets of cornflakes from a top shelf where they are otherwise out of reach. Unworthy of his calling? She thinks yes, but Basil when I put it to him will have none of it. Might not Jesus himself, he maintains, if so be he were area manager for a chain of small, self-service grocery and general stores in, as it might be, Ruislip, have not only condoned but even advocated the use of the crozier in some such way, as a means of achieving a significant increase in turnover? At the petrol pumps, as we read in the Scriptures, Jesus was after all very much alive to the necessity of increasing sales by all legitimate means.* Daphne remains unconvinced and stands her ground, citing one of the numerous stories related by Cardinal Wentworth in his *Background to Ecclesiastical History*. It transpires that in 1893 an Archbishop Witherington, catching sight whilst out walking of a somewhat personable young woman in difficulties on a horse – or in what he took to be difficulties on a horse – and rushing all too precipitately to her assistance, caught his foot in some brambles, tripped over his crozier in a hasty but doomed attempt to recover his balance, and was last seen, in the words of a bystander, to go 'arse over tip' in full canonicals down a slate quarry.

> His eventual arrival at the bottom minus his mitre and with his chasuble askew is something that engraves itself on the mind, but cannot be said to redound greatly to the credit of the episcopy or do any very signal service to the cause of organised religion.

It was a moment, in the opinion of many scholars, he goes on, when the fortunes of the church might be said to have reached their nadir. Over subsequent months he was to seek to justify so manifest an affront to orthodoxy on the grounds that his action

---

* I have been unable to find chapter and verse for this, though I let it pass at the time.

had been dictated by a need to bring much-needed publicity to the Church. Publicity, it has to be conceded, there certainly was, but of a kind such as the Church could, then as now, have readily dispensed with.

An issue, I suppose, that may never be fully resolved.

Dame Hettie 2

But Seriously – It's Sheila Hancock, BBC Two, 10 December 1972

Music and insurance. These two things are indissolubly linked in my mind, and it is to the large red building in Holborn that my imagination flies whenever the opening chords of Beethoven's Emperor Concerto start up…the Prudential Insurance Company's headquarters. For it was to this building as to a haven that my first husband was to come when in 1913 he arrived home after losing a thirty thousand pound contract as a result of getting locked in a lavatory in St Petersburg during the Russian winter of that time. But alas, the building was closed for the day, and it was not until, many years later, he found himself stuck in a lift in Siberia that he was finally to succeed in having himself insured against, as it turned out, tripping over a boulder on the banks of the Mississippi. It was his misfortune shortly after this to have a grand piano fall out of a removal van in Piccadilly onto his left foot. The piano, as a malign fate would have it, was on its way to the Albert Hall, where Sir Thomas Beecham, as he was at that time, was waiting on the rostrum with his baton raised to launch into the Emperor Concerto by Ludwig van Beethoven. A hot-blooded man, he was not accustomed to being kept waiting at a moment like that, for as with so many men when they have their baton poised, he was impatient to get started. A glance down at the pianist in front of him sitting there with no piano in front of him, was sufficient to tell him that some last-minute hitch had occurred. He stalked off the platform in rage, and frenzied activity went on behind the scenes to find some kind of substitute. Eventually they managed to find a spiritualist in the audience who was able to make contact with someone in the other world who claimed to have known Debussy at the height of his powers, and he was kind enough to lend them one of Tchaikovsky's old mouthorgans with the result that they were able to go on with Beethoven's Emperor Concerto almost as though nothing had happened. Had someone decided to go to court, there can be little doubt that my husband, the innocent victim in the affair, would have had not a leg to stand on. As indeed he hadn't, since it was underneath the piano, but it's a story which he begged me time and time again to tell on the air the moment television was invented in order that others might be spared the distress and anguish that the incident had caused.

Dame Hettie 3

But Seriously – It's Sheila Hancock, BBC Two, 31 December 1972

A complete guide to everything that the raw beginner could ever want to know about the art of embalming…this was the task dear Bernard and I set ourselves in the summer of that memorable year when people were at a loose end on a scale we have never experienced since. The hula hoop had not yet come in, the yo-yo was on its way out, and people were desperate for something to take its place. And sure enough it came. A craze which was to sweep the country like a prairie fire…alfresco embalming. Many people were doing wonders, but everywhere one saw the blunders that could so easily have been avoided if people could only be shown how to do it in the way the Ancient Egyptians did it, instead of relying on unreliable handbooks sold over the counter at Woolworths. We dropped everything and concentrated on producing *the* definitive manual covering everything from A to Z that the newly fledged alfresco embalmer could possibly need to know, and as a result popularised the ancient art as the ideal form of relaxation for those with time on their hands and loved ones to dispose of. Embalming parties were the really 'in' thing, of course, and for a time it was something that all London was doing until, quite suddenly, Munich, and the dark shadows of war were to put all thought of recreation from people's minds and for same reason the craze died and has never come to life again.

Dame Hettie 5

But Seriously – It's Sheila Hancock, BBC Two, 14 January 1973

As one looks back over the years at the many, many happy marriages one has been fortunate enough to contract, and at the many dear, dear men in whose fortunes one has been privileged to share so fully, one remembers with the greatest sense of sheer fun, I think, dear Lionel…whom one met and married when he was Deputy Governor of some small colonial island in India. He was putting down a rising of the natives there at the time we first came together, and he had just sent the ringleaders to Devil's Island or some such place, for five years. Later it came to light that he had, through some oversight, sentenced the wrong people! How we laughed! But with only a few short months of their sentence still to run, it hardly seemed worth going to the trouble of releasing them, and they were not to learn of their good fortune in receiving a complete pardon until they regained their freedom – but what a delightful piece of news to come home to! I mention this incident because in later years, as a High Court Judge, he was to make a similar mistake again. In another of those characteristic fits of absentmindedness he had donned the black cap and sentenced a man to death for riding his bicycle without lights. The sentence was carried out as quickly as possible to avoid publicity, but needless to say he had to put up with a good deal of good-natured ribbing from some of his fellow justices when they got to hear about it. True to his nature, he took it in very good part, and was as ready as anyone to see the joke against himself. Dear Lionel…

Private Eye #41, 12 July 1963

Escape

Untransmitted sketch for *But Seriously – It's Sheila Hancock*,
BBC Two, 31 December 1972

WOMAN 1
WOMAN 2
GEORGE

WOMAN 1: Dart club every Tuesday, and his pigeons at the weekends, it's not right. I never see him.

WOMAN 2: It's an escape.

WOMAN 1: And if he is home, all he does is paint his toy soldiers.

WOMAN 2: They live in a fantasy world.

WOMAN 1: He doesn't know half the time what's going on.

WOMAN 2: Can't face up to life as it really is, so they retreat into their own subconscious. Aristotle was the same. So was Descartes.

WOMAN 1: Who?

WOMAN 2: Life too much for them, so instead of darts they retreat into philosophy as an escape.

WOMAN 1: Yes.

WOMAN 2: To try and prove something to themselves.

WOMAN 1: I say to him sometimes – why on earth don't you put your soldiers away and stop turning your back on life all the time?

WOMAN 2: They do. Rembrandt was the same. They all do it. Yehudi Menuhin. The only reason he plays the violin is to try and prove to the world that he's not a window cleaner.

WOMAN 1: As if it mattered.

WOMAN 2: Well.

WOMAN 1: There's nothing wrong with being a window cleaner. Some of my best friends are window cleaners.

WOMAN 2: *But…*

WOMAN 1: It's not the kind of thing you want to shout from the housetops.

WOMAN 2: Or even admit to yourself.

WOMAN 1: Which is silly, because at heart he must *know.*

WOMAN 2: He knows, of course he knows but rather than face up to it and be the most outstanding window cleaner in the Western Hemisphere – as he could easily be if he put his mind to it – he prefers to wear out violin after violin in this desperate bid to keep the truth at bay at all costs.

WOMAN 1: It makes you want to go up to him and shake him, doesn't it? Be yourself, Yehudi Menuhin!

WOMAN 2: 'To thine ownself be true…thou canst not then be false to any man.'

WOMAN 1: Shakespeare, of course, he was another one.

WOMAN 2: I suppose we all *need* an escape. From time to time. It's when it takes over. Becomes permanent. A way of life.

WOMAN 1: Like that lot in there.

WOMAN 2: Where?

WOMAN 1: Balls Pond Road Cemetery.

WOMAN 2: Oh.

WOMAN 1: Running away from themselves all their lives until they end up in there wondering how they got there.

WOMAN 2: Yes.

WOMAN 1: *(Through window.)* Escape from that if you can!

    GEORGE looks in, holding darts.

GEORGE: Just off round the corner with Ted for some darts.

WOMAN 1: Have you made your will? Or is that something else you refuse to face up to? Is death just one more fact of life you turn your back on? Darts, darts, darts…you'd rather play darts with Ted, wouldn't you, than make provision for your family in the event of something happening to you! Just like the rest of them… Einstein, Plato, Tolstoy…you're all the same! Running away, running away…

GEORGE: *(Frozen in act of getting to hell out of it.)* God help me! I only wanted a game of darts!

The Fourth Dimension

Compilation One: Anatomy of Bewilderment, 2009.
Previously unpublished.

This isn't getting the universe explored, sir.

You're absolutely right, Bates.

Einstein country, here we come, sir.

Together we are about to open it up for civilisation, Bates.

It calls for great qualities, sir.

I have moments of weakness, Bates. Am I intrepid enough to explore the fourth dimension? I need to be told.

Oh, indeed, sir. The Livingstone of the space-time continuum, if I may say so, sir.

If you really think so.

I do, sir.

Right. Where do we go first?

We could make an initial sortie on to the lawn, sir, as a first step on our way into intergalactic space where we have reason to suppose the fourth dimension to be lurking.

Skulking would be a better word.

It would indeed, sir.

We'll run it to earth, Bates, if it's the last thing we do.

We certainly will, sir. We'll make it rue the day it was born. It'll be sorry it ever came kicking and squalling into the world.

Which way, Bates?

It doesn't matter, sir. Any direction will do.

Here's someone now who can direct us. Which way, pray, to the fourth dimension?

At this time? You'll be lucky! The fourth dimension'll have packed it in for the afternoon. It's eleven o'clock in the morning, for goodness sake.

What does he say, sir?

He says we'll be lucky if we get so much as a sniff of it, Bates.

Back to the drawing board then on this one, sir.

The Gift of Laughter

Private Eye #50, 15 November 1963

A Dredgekind and Grodmark Advertisement.

Issued on behalf of MORAL REARMAMENT

Laughter is something we can all indulge in. It is not a gift reserved for the favoured few. But unless our laughter is to be a mere empty hilarity, without aim or purpose, we must learn how to use it effectively. How many people know, for instance, that it was an ordinary laugh which was responsible for inflicting on the Russians one of the most devastating diplomatic defeats of the Cold War?

The story, which is quite true except for the facts, begins in 1954 when a well-known frogman working for NATO was suddenly suspected of Communist sympathies. Alarmed, he went to his doctor for a check-up. The X-ray, however, revealed nothing and eventually the suspicions disappeared. But the stigma remained.

A year or so later, an urgent call went out for experienced frogmen to be trained to laugh under water. Amongst the first to volunteer was the frogman who had been suspected less than two years before of Communist sympathies. He was auditioned, accepted, and sent for training. Six months later, and dripping wet, he was passed out. He could now, to use his own words, 'laugh like a gold-plated gridiron' at fifty fathoms.

Then the real test came. He was sent to the seabed off Vancouver Island with orders to laugh – not like a gold-plated gridiron, but like an empty cement mixer out of control. He did so. The laugh was then picked up 16,000 miles away on a privately owned radar screen, mistaken for the barking of a seal trapped under an ice floe in the Bering Straits, hurriedly dubbed into Russian by a team of six plain-clothes Egyptologists from the Sorbonne working round the clock, and re-transmitted on

26,000 megacycles in the direction of one of Soviet Russia's most powerful radio receiving stations.

It was a boldly conceived plan, calling for a high degree of co-ordination and for split-second timing. Had the Russians mistaken the sound for the barking of dogs, and had they deduced from this that the security forces of the West were engaged in training poodles to act as underwater bloodhounds somewhere off Nova Scotia, as was intended, they would have been compelled at all costs to devise immediate and effective countermeasures. Countermeasures which could well have involved diverting vital manpower from essential industries in order to experiment with yaks. Such a disorientation of the Soviet economy at that particular time would have constituted a major victory not only for the West, but for the frogman upon whose laugh the success of the whole enterprise would have depended.

The opportunity to laugh effectively on this level does not admittedly come to all of us every day. But how many of us would be ready for it if it did? How many of us would find that we had squandered the precious gift of laughter on things that were comic without being in any real sense important? And yet it is today more than ever that we need to recognise the necessity of disciplining ourselves – so that, whether in the struggle against Communism or in some other less spectacular way, our laughter is ready to play its part if ever the need should arise.

God's Whippet

Snippets Two, BBC Radio 3, 16 March 1983. Revised 2006.

It is not for nothing that St Thomas Aquinas, who was one of the fastest men the thirteenth century threw up, was known to his contemporaries as God's Whippet. It has been unfairly held against him that he was less than willing to give piggybacks to those who, late for an appointment, were not as fleet of foot. It's true that he would not give a piggyback to just anyone at a moment's notice. He reserved the right, and who shall blame him? The number of men of world stature who've been prepared to give piggybacks whenever they've been asked, and whether they were going in that direction in the first place or not, must be infinitesimal. Galileo, it is said, would rarely refuse if you were really desperate, and Richelieu was known as a soft touch in this area, if you knew how to put your case. But such choice spirits are rare indeed. Usually, as with Clive of India, you had to choose your moment. Where Aquinas stands out, however, is that he was able, not only to give people piggybacks, provided he received some sort of notice in advance, but to prove the existence of God at the same time. As anyone who has ever tried it will confirm, proving the existence of God is difficult enough at the best of times. But to do it with someone weighing ten or fifteen stone on your back is, you might think, well-nigh impossible. And yet Aquinas was able to do it not once but five times in succession, with only a short break in between. It is a record that has yet to be beaten, though attempt after attempt has been made. The best showing was Cardinal Newman, who is said to have managed it three times before giving up on doctor's orders when he started getting palpitations. It is tempting to say that if he was under the doctor, he was unwise even to contemplate proving the existence of God but, to my mind, it is a measure of the man that, notwithstanding the risks, he was ready to have a go. I admire Aquinas, as who does not? But I take off my hat to Newman, even though, pleading a weak heart, he refused point-blank to give piggybacks to anyone other than members of his family, and then only on Bank Holidays.

The Grave My Silencer

The Lodestone, Birkbeck College, Spring 1954

Although Private Toomey had an easier time of it than I had when it came to getting the upper-hand of a motorcycle, it probably took more out of him in the end. Nothing Sergeant Broadrib ever had us all doing caused Toomey the same distress of mind as the things we might possibly be having to do next. With me it was quite the other way. The fear that tomorrow we might be riding single file round the rim of a blast furnace hardly troubled me at all as I went hurtling down one slagheap and up the next.

What Toomey experienced on the mental plane was more than matched by pretty nearly everything I went through on the physical. It generally got put down to my reflexes, though never by Sergeant Broadrib. As there was precious little the matter with Sergeant Broadrib's reflexes, he very likely looked on mine as a form of malingering.

It often seemed to me that Broadrib understood more about our machines than he did about us. Or than we did about either. In spite of that he was an excellent instructor who, so it was said, could be thoroughly caustic in his abuse without ever arousing rancour. Even those of us who had difficulty in telling where one ended and the other began had to agree that it was a fine gift to have. Or even to be thought of as having.

I can see now that I ought to have been far more disheartened than I was by his incredible feats of motorcycling skill. Those who had the sense to be thoroughly disheartened by them on the first day out got off on the whole fairly lightly. At least he never got as nettled about their kick-starters as he did about mine.

'It isn't *on* that side for crissake!'

In the end he more or less gave me up. We gave each other up in a way. Not that our relationship had done much except founder from the start.

'On the whole,' I remarked once, smiling gingerly, 'it's played a pretty minor part, all this sort of thing, in my way of life.'

Without taking his eyes off me, he put a cigarette between his lips and felt for his matches.

'Till now,' he said.

Shortly after that I got rid of my front brake. It was ripped off in one of the two or three quarries at the top of which I was supposed to have brought my machine to a halt. I shall not go so far as to pretend that I had no idea what the front brake was for, but it was obvious that the loss of it was going to make very little difference to me. Sergeant Broadrib seemed to see it in much the same light. He silently wound the trailing cable round my handle-bar and waved me on. As I went I noticed him putting the brake lever into his pannier; perhaps to him it was a symbol of something or other.

At moments of crisis like that I have a fortunate knack of standing right outside myself and weighing my own reactions with cool detachment. No one else seemed to be able to do that, least of all Private Toomey. Perhaps he was afraid that once out he would never be able to get back in again. It would certainly have matched up well enough with some of his other fears, such as that Broadrib was out to humiliate him by having us all riding through the streets of Halifax in gasmasks. It was his native city.

We did, as it turned out, have to ride a couple of miles wearing gasmasks, though not in Halifax. It was not a very alarming experience for those whose eyepieces had been properly smeared with anti-dim beforehand. Mine, which had not, quickly began clouding over on the inside. Soon I was riding blind. It was a nasty enough situation even for one who to all intents and purposes had been riding blind since the course started; for anyone else it must almost certainly have ended in disaster.

Nothing, I suppose, could ever have got as distorted as some of these things obviously have, without having been pretty incredible to begin with. No less incredible in its own way is the fact that within three weeks I was passed out as a dispatch rider. One week more and I expect they would have made me an instructor. Fortunately I never had to go near a motorcycle again.

I Could Have Died

But Seriously – It's Sheila Hancock, BBC Two, 14 January 1973

CONSULTANT
....

PATIENT
....

Whitecoated medical CONSULTANT with PATIENT.

PATIENT has long, lugubrious face suffused with sepulchral gloom.

CONSULTANT: What exactly is it about the world that you find so irresistibly funny, Mr Bayswater?

PATIENT: Everything. The whole circus. The whole ludicrous set-up. It's pure farce from beginning to end.

CONSULTANT: And this is at the root of your urge to fall about laughing.

PATIENT: Yes.

CONSULTANT: And yet you steadfastly resist the urge.

PATIENT: I laugh inwardly.

CONSULTANT: You've never done it out loud?

PATIENT: No, thank you very much!

CONSULTANT: Your fear of rupturing yourself seems to have a pretty powerful effect on you.

PATIENT: So it would you if you had my sense of humour.

CONSULTANT: Yes…

PATIENT: Besides which, I don't hold with the vulgarity of it. I happen to believe it's rude to laugh in public, and in front of other people. It's not…the thing.

CONSULTANT: You laugh, as it were, inside you.

PATIENT: *(Taps head.)* In here. I enjoy a good joke in here.

CONSULTANT: You're probably falling about at this very moment, in fact.

PATIENT: Oh yes. I hardly ever stop. It's one long giggle. If it's not one thing, it's another. It's a pretty hilarious old world, when you come down to it.

CONSULTANT: Yes…

CONSULTANT turns to camera as we move in, losing PATIENT, for the confidential man-to-man hardsell.

CONSULTANT: … This man is clearly a fool, but he shares his problem with many other people who, like him, are gifted with a keen sense of humour but are afraid to let themselves go for fear of the consequences. In a laughter-conscious age, laughter fatigue is an ever-present danger…and it is for this reason that we have brought out the Proxy Proxymatic Electronic Laughtermaster…small enough to fit into your coat pocket, yet powerful enough to provide the complete answer to all your laughter chores…

Lugubrious PATIENT with Laughtermaster fitted in top pocket.

CONSULTANT: … No more aching sides, no more uncomfortable doubling up, no more disfiguring tears of laughter, as the Laughtermaster takes over…you can give full rein to gloom and despondency without leaving the chair you are sitting in.

Laughtermaster adjusted by fingertip control has been gently chuckling away and now rises to loud maniac laughter as gloomy PATIENT's face takes on for first time a contented half-smile of satisfaction.

Fade.

I know it's not a fashionable thing to say these days, but you don't have to go far to see the hoof of a Dartmoor pony imprinted on most of your present-day crimes.

Dartmoor ponies've got a lot to answer for. Always have had.

Murders in the Rue Morgue. Jack the Ripper. Marie Celeste. Pony hoofmarks all over them.

A lot of people dismiss it as a load of nonsense, of course. Which is why they go on getting away with it.

Compilation One: Anatomy of Bewilderment, 2009. Previously unpublished.

The Insomnia Case

Birkbeck College, c.1955

Private Gold suffered from sleeplessness at night and so was hardly ever awake during the day, but otherwise we were all up and about. When she could spare the time to see to it matron liked to have us occupied as well. We knew it irritated and unsettled her to come round with sister and find us in little wicker armchairs playing draughts or reading *The Hound of the Baskervilles*, but once she took us by surprise.

'It's the same thing in here, sister.'

In the act of getting hurriedly to his feet Private Toomey had been trapped between chair and table in the anguished posture of a bent nail.

'Instead of all exercising their limbs as much as they can.'

We tried to look like people who have just sent out for more floor-polish.

'They just stand there, all of them, and expect to get better.'

Soon there were tasks for all and some to spare, but at Toomey with his arms in plaster she was brought up short.

'We ought to be able to find something. A man like you with strong, healthy legs. What are they doing in the office, sister? Perhaps he could call out numbers for them.'

On her way out matron caught sight of a bedcover and paused to see it straightened. Under it Private Gold lay to attention with his eyes closed.

'The insomnia case,' remarked sister.

It was the job of the nurse on duty to rouse him at the proper times for his sleeping tablets, but although he sat up for meals he never fully came round till lights out. After that he reckoned to lie awake till it was time to sit up for breakfast.

The day I arrived they told him he was being sent back to his unit. He took it with cynical composure.

'That's what it does to them,' he explained. 'That's the military mind for you.'

They gave him a travel warrant and told him to report to the company office on arrival. Two days later he was back.

In the end he asked for an interview with the padre, who was shown in by matron and came up to each of us in turn; we paused in our dusting to talk uneasily about this and that for a few moments while matron stood by and the constraint built up, until at last he reached the bed where Private Gold was sitting up, impatient to be done with irrelevancies.

'I don't feel I'm getting anywhere, padre.'

Someone brought a chair.

'It's not so much the sleeplessness as psychological.'

After his interview he slept through till lights out and then woke Toomey explaining how dreams can be responsible for a subconscious fear of sleep.

We were awakened shortly after midnight; the lights were on and Private Gold was allowing himself to be given a sedative. Stepping back with the glass in his hand, the night orderly stood and watched it take effect.

'Psychobloodyparalysed,' he said. 'That's what he wants.'

Soon the lights were out and the ward was quiet again. We lay for some time listening to the deep, even breathing of Private Gold, and then one by one we too fell asleep.

Interview

Compilation One: Anatomy of Bewilderment, 2009.
Previously unpublished.

I wonder if you could tell me, broadly speaking, what you look like.

Oh…

Tall. Short. Fat. Thin. It's just for the record. And so that we can have some sort of mental picture of the kind of person we're dealing with.

Well…

Shoulders, for example. How many of those, all told?

Just the two, really.

Good. Both arms roughly the same length, I imagine.

As near as dammit.

Not a dwarf, or anything of that ilk…

Not to my knowledge, no.

Eskimo at all?

No.

Have you ever *been* an Eskimo?

Not to my recollection.

What about distinguishing marks? Beard. Tattoos. That sort of thing.

Not on me, no.

Head for heights at all?

No. I get dizzy just standing on the ground!

Head for figures, perhaps.

No. Definitely not!

You make the same one do for everything, in other words.

Well…yes… I suppose I do.

Right. I think that's more or less it…except for one last thing – rather important! – where could we find you?

Find me?

At the present moment. If we wanted to get in touch.

Well… I'm here…actually. Sitting in front of you.

Fine. It's just so that we can know where to look in case we should have to contact you about anything.

Introduction to 'The Hole'

Writers' Theatre (Heinemann Educational Books, 1967).
The accompanying extract from the 1958 play *The Hole* is not included in the present volume, but can be found on p.149-158 of *Collected Plays* (Faber and Faber, 2013).

This is a passage from a play I wrote some little time ago, when I was thinking about the way we have to weave all kinds of elaborately significant myths around the hard facts of existence, before we can begin to come to terms with the world as a place to live in; often, in the process, reaching the point where we believe much more implicitly in the myth, than in the facts, historical or otherwise, on which the myth is supposed to be based.

In the play, to represent the hard facts of existence at their most prosaic and mundane, there is a hole in the road with a workman at the bottom of it doing something to an electric cable; and there are passers-by stopping every now and again to watch. But as the hole goes down quite a long way, it isn't at all easy to make out, in the semi-darkness at the bottom, what it is that's going on down there. The only man, in fact, who has no doubts whatever about it is the one who from his vantage point at the edge of the hole, where he has taken up his position with food and blankets, is sure he can see preparations being made for the solemn unveiling of the great window in the south transept. He expects it to be an awe-inspiring spectacle.

What the others see, or think they see, though no less far-fetched, is to begin with much more matter-of-fact and commonplace. A game of what appears to be table tennis; someone trying to play golf; a tank with fish swimming about in it. But in the course of the talk and argument these things give rise to, we find them gradually beginning to gather round them all kinds of new and unsuspected subtleties of meaning. Simply by virtue of being talked about they take on a profound significance such as they never had on their account, and end by arousing feelings which are held with such passionate intensity that they can be expressed only in ritualized action, as they are in the passage printed here.

Of the people involved in this episode, Soma is the one who in various guises throughout the play represents power and authority; Cerebro is the thinker – the man whose ideas Soma takes up and instinctively puts into the form in which they can best be used to seduce everyone, including Soma himself and Cerebro, into behaving as Soma for the moment thinks they should; and Endo is the ordinary man, anxious to do and say and think the right thing, but never somehow as sure how to go about it as either Soma or Cerebro always manage to give the appearance of being. And there are the two women, fully occupied with lesser and more practical matters, but ready – without thinking much about it one way or the other – to do whatever is required of them when the occasion demands.

In the play, as in life, everything that happens seems to arise out of something as casual and random as the encounter with which this passage begins. Here the throwing down of a fork like a spent match suddenly for no apparent reason triggers off a chain reaction. Within minutes the men are caught up in a wave of mass hysteria, which sweeps them along, generating its own momentum as it goes, and carrying all before it. In the wild confusion of the climax, we see human beings going frantically haywire like mechanisms out of control.

When this has finally played itself out, and been disposed of by Soma's abrupt change of mood in the music-hall cross-talk act with Endo, reality returns in the form of cold, sober fact. There is just a junction-box, three or four cables, and a workman carrying out repairs to them.

Perhaps it is hardly necessary for me to add that in no time at all a new religion, based on 'the ever-lasting electricity' and 'The Excavation of the Rectangular Cavity', has begun to take shape almost of its own volition. Before long it has reached the full flower of maturity; and by the end of the play, since what we make of reality matters more to us than reality itself, everyone except the man who is waiting for the great window in the south transept to be unveiled has embraced it, with all the naturalness of a child falling asleep, as the only true faith.

J.C. Mulligan

Ambit #202, October 2010

Finally, in the wake of heavy hints from all quarters about freeing up some space on this grotesquely overcrowded planet, a relic just unearthed of my brief stint as obituarist on *The Times*:

J. C. Mulligan, whom I knew as both friend and one-time colleague, was a remarkable character. Always a protean figure, he was a passionate believer in the revitalising power of metamorphosis. Polymorphism indeed was his life. Paperclip, gantry, ormolu clock, candlewick bedspread, glasshouse – these are but a few of his myriad manifestations. On the occasion of our first meeting he was a chainlink fence. He had been a peahen a year or two before, but something caused him to take a dislike to the life and he went off to Somerset to become an antimacassar. Antimacassars were very much in favour just then, and he was soon changing hands at prices which to me in those days would have been a small fortune. Shortly after that he went back to being a paperclip, and in fact was never again to command so high a price as he had during those halcyon days as an antimacassar. I saw little of him while he was a paperclip. It was not until he branched out for the first time as an ormolu clock that I became really intimate with him. We saw a great deal of each other, both while he was on loan to the Wallace Collection and later when he went to America, because as luck would have it we were to be living within a few hundred yards of one another almost from the moment we landed. My own job was one which left me free in the afternoons, and so we could often be seen strolling along Fifth Avenue together somewhere between three and four in the afternoon – four o'clock being the time he had to get back on to the small shelf where he worked during the evening. I wondered, when he became a peahen for the second time, how far his earlier experiences were going to modify and shape his outlook on things. I knew, for instance, that there had been an episode on the former occasion about which he was reluctant to say very much, but which I learned from those who knew him at the time had something to do with a peacock. It was all rather vague, and no one seemed at all sure of the details, but from what I could piece together there was some kind of liaison involving a peacock and another peahen. Whatever the facts of the matter were, he left very soon afterwards and got a job as a candlewick bedspread in a country hotel somewhere and spent what he described to me afterwards as some of the happiest days of his somewhat chequered life. The work was not arduous – it was summer – and a great deal of the time he was free to do very much as he liked. His friends saw something of him when he came up for a few days, but his time seems to have been pretty fully occupied. It was at about this time that he became friendly with an eiderdown – some would say too friendly! – and was paying some kind of court to a counterpane as well if rumour is to be believed. But he was the kind of person around whom gossip always seems to circulate and it isn't always possible to say how much of it was exaggerated, how much slightly apocryphal and how much pure fabrication.

Mulligan was, in every sense of the word, a rolling stone, gathering such moss as he could in the occasional brief interval between bouts of rolling. He was a notoriously bad hand at looking after it once gathered however. It was a standing joke among his friends that whenever you called on him he would be trying conscientiously but not very successfully to 'do something', as he put it, about his moss. He toyed with the idea of having it painted green in the interests of verisimilitude – of a kind! – but never took it up as a serious proposition as far as I can remember. Nor would it have done more than disguise the ravages of time and neglect his moss was almost invariably suffering from.

He will be particularly missed by the park bench, the small Jacobean snuff box and the set of brass stair-rods which were his constant companions during his later years.

He is survived by a boxed edition of the Complete Works of Sir Walter Scott.

Leibnitz and
the Boot Cupboard

Snippets Two, BBC Radio 3, 15 March 1983. Revised 2006.

How many of us have ever paused to reflect on the debt we owe to Sir Isaac Newton? He it was who discovered gravity and it is salutary to reflect that, but for him, we might still be looking. Leibnitz is another to whom we are more indebted than we always care to acknowledge. Out in all weathers looking for the infinitesimal calculus, and refusing to let up until he finally ran it to earth. He became very much the popular hero as a result of it, and the scenes of wild rejoicing that greeted the news of his success have become very much the stuff of legend. 'It's been found! The infinitesimal calculus has been found!' And among the crowd who carried him shoulder-high through the streets were some who could remember vividly the day it went missing. Large as life one moment. Hide nor hair the next. It was a mystery to rival that of the Mary Celeste. Small wonder there were those who had serious doubts whether it would ever be seen again. It was then that Leibnitz, rummaging through an old boot and shoe cupboard for a pair of galoshes he knew were around somewhere but couldn't remember where, spotted something in a corner and took a torch to it. For some moments, he was scarcely able to credit the evidence of his senses, for there, crouching down behind a roll of linoleum and swathed in curtain material, hoping thereby to be mistaken for Henry Irving in *A Midsummer Night's Dream*, was the very infinitesimal calculus he had spent so many months and years vainly looking for. He could hardly believe his luck. 'You are the infinitesimal calculus!' he shouted, absolutely delirious with excitement. Sensing the game was up, out it came, blinking, into the sunlight and it was the work of a moment to snap handcuffs on to it and take it to the headquarters of the Royal Society for forensic tests to determine its age by means of carbon dating before placing it on show in the Natural History Museum for future generations to wonder at.

Leslie Cricklehurst

World in Ferment, BBC Two, 21 July 1969

NANCY CHUFF

LESLIE CRICKLEHURST

NANCY: In Xanadu did Kubla Khan
             A stately pleasure-dome decree:
             Where Alph, the sacred river, ran
             Through caverns measureless to man
             Down to a sunless sea.

These words were written by Samuel Taylor Coleridge a hundred and seventy-two years ago. Coleridge himself died in 1834, but here in the studio with me is Mr Leslie Cricklehurst…

We go to LESLIE CRICKLEHURST. He is dressed to resemble Napoleon.

NANCY: …who claims as a spare-time hobby to be the reincarnation not only of Samuel Taylor Coleridge, but of W.B. Yeats and other famous names as well. He is also a keen practitioner of the art of shoe salesmanship. How much time, in fact, does this leave you for other things?

LESLIE: Other things…?

NANCY: Such as cleaning your teeth.

LESLIE: Well, tooth-cleaning does actually take very much a back seat so far as priorities are concerned. First things first – and in my own considered opinion, it's my reincarnation work that must essentially get the lion's share of what time is going once I've sold the required quota of footwear for the day in question.

NANCY: In other words you do your reincarnation after the day's work is over.

LESLIE: Yes, well I get in and have a wash and my tea, and then I go straight up and…

NANCY: Yes. How, in point of fact, did you come to take up reincarnation in the first place?

LESLIE: It was by accident, really. I was wandering lonely as a cloud one day down Shoreditch way, and I suddenly saw this crowd of golden daffodils.

NANCY: Fluttering and dancing in the breeze.

LESLIE: Fluttering and dancing in the breeze. So I thought – Hallo. What's up here? Anyway, I didn't say anything till I got home, and then when we were sitting round the table having our supper I came out with it. I said, 'I must see these daffodils.' They said, 'What daffodils?' I said, 'Down Shoreditch.' So then Myrtle chimed in – she's my sister – she said, 'I suppose you were wandering lonely as a cloud?' So I said, 'Yes, as a matter of fact.' And it was then that I realised I was the reincarnation of Wordsworth.

NANCY: Yes, I see. And…

LESLIE: And then as luck would have it my Uncle Bert, who was really William Blake but had had to take on Tennyson as well at short notice because the other chap who was normally Tennyson was off sick at the time, suddenly dropped down dead in the middle of 'The Charge of the Light Brigade' at a pub in Sheen. So naturally they turned to me. And then one thing led to another.

NANCY: And now you're the reincarnation of no fewer than… four hundred and fifty-three different literary figures. Is this a record so far as reincarnation is concerned?

LESLIE: It's not strictly a world record, because there's someone in Ecuador who claims to be able to top it, but we're disputing that and it's going before the international tribunal next year, which I'm hoping will decide in my favour.

NANCY: Us too. Our final question. Before we came on to the programme we were discussing the lines I quoted a few moments ago –

> Where Alph, the sacred river, ran
> Through caverns measureless to man.

How measureless to man, frankly, were they – in your experience as Samuel Taylor Coleridge?

LESLIE: Well… I couldn't measure them. Put it that way.

NANCY: Not even with…

LESLIE: Not even with an echo sounder.

NANCY: Which, of course, hadn't been invented then.

LESLIE: Hundred and fifty years too early.

NANCY: Thank you, Leslie Cricklehurst, and good luck in your career as well as your hobby.

Letter to Private Eye

Private Eye #199, 1 August 1969

Sir: I have been asked by friends to add
my small mite to the argument that has been
raging in your columns over the last five
or six weeks - or if not in your columns,
in the columns of some other journal with
which I must for some reason be confusing
it - about the caterpillar tracks said to
have been discovered in 1789 at Pompeii.
Much of value has been said on both sides
as to the genuineness or otherwise of
Professor Mortlake's claim that these were
left by hordes of marauding caterpillars
in the fifth century B.C. as they streamed
in from as far afield as what is now eastern Siberia. My own views on the matter,
however, are by now I think sufficiently
well known, and I have no wish to try the
patience of your readers by prolonging
still further a controversy which may well
have been going on for far too long already. I would therefore beg leave simply
to sign myself: Yours etc, Hugh Latimer
Brasenose-Smith.

   Yours etc,
    N. F. SIMPSON

(Permission granted. Ed)

(Most grateful. N.F.S.)

   Yours etc,
  HUGH LATIMER BRASENOSE-SMITH

Sir:

I have been asked by friends to add my small mite to the argument that has been raging in your columns over the last five or six weeks – or if not in your columns, in the columns of some other journal with which I must for some reason be confusing it – about the caterpillar tracks said to have been discovered in 1789 at Pompeii. Much of value has been said on both sides as to the genuineness or otherwise of Professor Mortlake's claim that these were left by hordes of marauding caterpillars in the fifth century B.C. as they streamed in from as far afield as what is now eastern Siberia. My own views on the matter, however, are by now I think sufficiently well known, and I have no wish to try the patience of your readers by prolonging still further a controversy which may well have been going on for far too long already. I would therefore beg leave simply to sign myself: Yours etc, Hugh Latimer Brasenose-Smith.

Yours etc,

N.F. SIMPSON

(Permission granted. Ed)

(Most grateful. N.F.S.)

Yours etc,

HUGH LATIMER BRASENOSE-SMITH

Making Nonsense
of Nonsense

Transatlantic Review #21, Summer 1966

The moment N.F. Simpson came into the room, looking gaunt
and haggard, I weighed in with my first question.

Q: You have been described as a man who is at odds with a
completely unidentifiable experience that for twenty-three
hours out of the twenty-four goes clanging and thundering
along on his stream of consciousness like a mobile iron
foundry out of control. Is this a fair statement of your
dilemma?

A: What dilemma?

We fell silent for twenty-five minutes or so. Eventually, by way of
keeping the ball in the air, I asked him about his latest play, *The
Cresta Run.*

Q: Your latest play, *The Cresta Run,* doesn't appear to have had a
very favourable reception from the critics.

A: No.

Q: They didn't seem to find it very funny.

A: No.

Q: Was this deliberate, do you think?

A: Oh, yes. Quite deliberate. They went out of their way.
There's no question about that.

Q: What about other people? The ordinary playgoers. Did they
find it funny?

A: Not particularly.

Q: I see. And yet the extraordinary thing that arises out of all
this is that you've actually put on weight.

A: Only five and a half ounces.

Q: It's better than nothing.

A: I suppose it is.

Q: For someone of your build.

At this point the conversation ranged over a wide field, and I was able to bring it back to the matter in hand only by asking a direct question of a rather personal nature. What the hell, I said, happened to that pair of exquisitely fashioned mayonnaise and tomato ketchup pourers you were telling everybody you picked up for a song in Old Kent Road two years ago last Christmas? He looked at me through eyes which had narrowed to mere slits. It wasn't a song, he said, snarlingly, it was the Tibetan National Anthem.

Q: In that case, perhaps you can tell me the answer to a cognate question. The ideas in your plays – some of them are remarkable for being fantastic and far-fetched to an altogether astonishing degree. We have had someone teaching weighing machines to sing the Hallelujah Chorus from Handel's Messiah, a man building a full-size replica of the Old Bailey, which is the Central Criminal Court of London, in his suburban living room, and conducting a full-scale trial there; we have had people getting sent an elephant which turns out when it arrives to be the wrong size, and finding themselves saddled with a pair of comedians who commandeer the kitchen for a cross-talk act and then expect to be given coffee and biscuits afterwards; and we've had…

A: Yes. All right. What about it?

Q: Well – where do you get these ideas *from*?

A: Oh…

He thought for several moments, then shrugged.

A: They come and go.

Q: But where do they come from?

A: They just turn up.

Q: But surely…

A: They don't consult me.

Q: No, possibly not, but…

A: They're in and out as the whim takes them.

Q: I see.

A: Half of them I've never even seen.

Q: In other words you have no control over them at all?

A: I give one or other of them a bit of a look sometimes, but on the whole they treat me as if I were the doorman.

Q: You never, I suppose, venture out in search of ideas?

A: Venture *out*?

Q: Yes. I wondered…

A: You must be mad!

Q: For ideas outside the…

A: They'd have the bailiffs in before I'd turned the corner!

Q: You really think they would?

A: That lot? They wouldn't hesitate.

Q: Good gracious.

I asked Mr Simpson what it was that he always kept uppermost in his mind when writing his plays.

A: I'm very glad you asked me that.

Neither of us spoke for some time.

Q: Is it perhaps what someone once called 'the absent-minded irony of fate at work amongst us – turning stately farce into knockabout tragedy'?

A: Yes.

Q: Who, in fact, did say that?

A: I did.

Q: And didn't you also refer at the same time to what you called 'grave, censorious, senatorial, soul-possessing Man, erect on his two spindles'?

A: No.

Q: Oh. I thought you did.

A: No.

Q: I must be thinking of someone else.

A: You are.

Q: Who?

A: Dylan Thomas.

As we chatted, it soon became apparent that, for what it was worth, Mr Simpson's opinion of God was not all that much higher than his opinion of Man. When I asked him why he nevertheless continued to believe, unlike so many of his contemporaries, in the existence of a Supreme Being, his reply was simple and to the point. Who else, he said, could have boobed on that kind of scale?

Q: On the other hand, in all fairness, you've got to remember that if it's the creation we're talking about, this is an event which took place some five thousand million years or more ago, at a time when the kind of resources that are available today for an enterprise as ambitious as that were still very much a thing of the distant future.

A: True.

Q: We've got devices at our disposal today that would have turned God green with envy back at the time of Genesis.

A: I'm sure.

Q: He'd have given his eye-teeth for them.

A: He would.

Q: In those crucial initial stages.

A: No doubt about it.

Q: An absolute godsend to him.

A: Absolute.

We pursued the subject far into the night, until at length I put the question that had been niggling at me since early the previous afternoon.

Q: And yet, despite all this, you turn a decidedly disenchanted eye on any form of scientific achievement. Why?

For a good three hours, Mr Simpson stood staring out of the window, deep in thought.

Q: Is what you are trying to say simply, perhaps, this: That science has maimed us as human beings by leaving us with only five senses to do the work of six?

A: Yes.

Q: And that you are appalled at the spectacle of us all bashing away with spanner and monkey wrench at the age-old mysteries of the universe, like some dementedly slap-happy bomb disposal squad dismantling a landmine?

A: Yes.

We again fell silent, and I began edging my way to the door.

A: Where are *you* off to?

Q: I…thought I'd slip upstairs and run myself a bath.

A: Oh.

Q: If that's all right.

At the bathroom door I heard someone calling up.

A: Use the pink towel.

Q: Right.

A: The one on the left.

When we resumed, Mr Simpson was in more expansive mood.

A: The exercise of a perpetual and all-encompassing derision – that's the crying need at this particular point in the world's history.

Q: Yes?

A: In my opinion.

Q: Yes. To come back to your plays…

A: It's the only hope.

Q: You think it is?

A: For mankind.

Q: Yes. You may well be right.

A: To recognise, before it's too late, the one paramount need – which is to cut ourselves down to size.

Q: To come back to your…

A: By every means in our power.

Q: Yes. I'm sure.

A: And at every possible opportunity.

Q: To come back to your plays. You once said that your plays 'can be readily understood by anyone who has ever been threaded through the top of somebody else's pyjama trousers, and found himself protruding from both ends at once.' Would you still go along with this assessment of your work?

A: In part.

Q: Which part?

A: It doesn't really matter. Any part.

Q: I see.

We looked at each other guardedly for a moment or two.

Q: Would you care to enlarge on that at all?

A: No.

In a sense we were back at square one; in another sense, we had covered far more ground than either of us had dared at the outset to hope.

Q: If I could move on now to something else, I should like to ask you about your attitude to words.

A: Words?

Q: Yes. The tools of your trade, as it were.

A: Christ.

Q: You once said that you would hate to be mistaken for 'the kind of writer through whose lucid prose one is conducted like a distinguished visitor from thought to thought, until the itinerary being at length complete, one cannot but have arrived.'

A: Is that what I said?

Q: And that 'nothing is more euphoric than this profound sense of arrival – or more bogus.'

A: I've got a vague memory…

Q: 'A closing cadence,' you went on, 'is the oldest confidence trick of them all – knowing all the time, as one does, that there is scarcely a statement one can make that does not slip bit by bit with every word further and further from what to begin with showed every promise of encompassing some simple, serviceable truth.'

A: Protean.

Q: What is?

A: Truth.

Q: I see what you mean. Yes. Not a bad word for it. On the whole.

A: Bit of a flux.

Q: It is. It is indeed.

A: When you get down to it.

Q: Slips through your fingers before you've had time to look round.

A: Very devil to pin down.

Q: Nightmare.

A: Like following life through creatures we dissect, really.

Q: It is.

A: We lose it in the moment we detect.

Q: Quite. Quite. You never said a truer word.

A: Somebody else said it, actually.

Q: Knew his onions, whoever he was.

A: Pope.

Q: Oh?

A: To be exact.

Q: Well, well.

A: *Moral Essays.* Epistle One.

Q: Oh, yes.

A: To Sir Richard Temple, Lord Cobham.

Q: Aha.

A: 1733, or thereabouts.

Q: Yes?

A: Lines twenty-nine and thirty.

Q: Well.

A: Credit where it's due.

Q: Absolutely.

It was at this point in our interview that I suggested to Mr Simpson that he might like to pose for one or two photographs, and we broke off to scour the neighbourhood for a suitable camera at the kind of price he felt like paying. It came to nothing, however, and we took up again where we'd left off.

Q: To come back to the question of words. Would you agree, by and large, that words which in their own right and on the page are meaningless, or have a meaning which is trivial or irrelevant, may nevertheless produce a strong undertow of emotional significance when spoken in a given situation?

A: Well…

Q: And that very often, both in plays and in life, things are going on which need words not to explain them, but to give them substances and texture?

A: It's on the cards, I suppose.

Q: That conversation, in fact, is less a means of communication than a mode of behaviour; and that in practice language is a much more neutral medium than the theatre, partly by its very nature, has tended to make it seem.

A: Well…

Q: I haven't finished.

A: Oh.

Q: So that one tends to think of communication between people as being dependent on their capacity for exchanging information and ideas by means of words, as though a rich vocabulary and a good command of syntax were all that was necessary to enable us to make contact with one another. And as though people who have no particular gift for using words are thereby in some way prevented from entering into a close harmony with other people as inarticulate as themselves.

A: It doesn't make sense, does it?

Q: You'll have your turn in a minute, *I'm* asking the questions.

A: Carry on.

Q: As though, in so far as words play a part in communications at all on any level other than that of a mere intellectual transaction, it were the words themselves, and their meaning, that mattered. When it is palpably obvious that what matters is the act of speaking. And the way that act is carried out. And the moment chosen for it. And the context of other activities and feelings in which it takes place.

A: Yes.

Q: And would you agree that words which are fulfilling this kind of function in a play, could also be chosen by the playwright in such a way as to have a meaning of their own, which could make sense independently of the action of the play, though in harmony with it?

A: Yes, I think…

Q: Forming a kind of descant, in fact, over what might be called the melodic line of the play.

A: In a sense.

Q: Syphoning off, as it were, the surplus meaning, and harnessing it for purposes of his own.

A: Yes. I think I'd go along with that.

Q: Perhaps to make some kind of oblique comment, perhaps for comic effect, perhaps for both.

A: Absolutely.

Q: The comic effect being at its most powerful when the line or sense, or nonsense, carried along in the words is totally at odds with everything else that is going on in the play at the time they are spoken.

A: Oh, yes. That goes without saying.

Q: Good.

A: Oh, yes.

Q: It doesn't make much sense to me, but as long as you're happy.

I asked Mr Simpson if there was any advice or help he could give to playgoers who were deeply concerned to understand his plays, but were at something of a loss to know how to go about it.

A: Advice?

Q: As to stance or posture in the theatre, for instance.

A: I see.

Q: Or any other help.

A: Yes. I'm trying to think.

Q: We haven't got all day.

A: How would it be…?

Q: Yes?

A: How would it be if I issued it in the form of a statement?

Q: *Any* form. As long as we get it.

A: Let me put it this way, then. Various semantic, philosophical, and metaphysical ideas have with varying degrees of ingenuity been profitably keyed into my plays by those with a bent for it.

On the other hand, audiences who try to get down to it with pencil and paper while the thing's actually going on in front of them, are likely to have a thinner time of it by and large than the ones who breeze into the theatre in a mood of genial scepticism, and rely simply on a working knowledge of where the exits are in case of need.

Q: Flood, you mean? Or famine.

A: Well…yes. Yes.

We talked on. Eventually, after two or three months of it, I put one final question to Mr Simpson.

Q: If I might put one final question to you, Mr Simpson. You are on record as having said that your aim in writing plays was to coax a grudging suspension of disbelief out of a wary audience, in the firm conviction that what we all need is to be inoculated against lunacy by means of small doses of some comparatively mild strain, in order to build up a resistance to the dreadful and destructive ravages of that most terrible of all known forms, which goes by the name of sanity.

A: That was part of a remark made under duress several years ago.

Q: Oh?

A: In a siren suit at Weybridge.

Q: I see.

It seemed hardly within the bounds of good taste to pursue the question any further, but I did. Would you have made the same remark under the same circumstances if it had been someone else who was under duress instead of you? Mr Simpson thought for a moment, and then turned to me with his most engaging smile. There you have me, he said.

BE IN AT YOUR
OWN DEATH

leisure promotions
offers a unique experience

To those who want to
GET OUT OF THE RUT

Have you ever imagined
the thrill of being on
trial for your life ?

Here at last - the ULTIMATE in involvement !

you have been framed by experienced ex-crooks acting on
instructions from LEISURE PROMOTIONS. You are being
led into the dock for the first time. At first you feel bewilderment and a kind of heady excitement. Then, as the trial
runs its slow but inexorable course, a dull, aching tedium
begins to spread over you. Suddenly you are brought with a
sharp jolt back to reality; the jury are withdrawing to consider their verdict. A long and agonising wait and at last
they return. Almost at once a numbing wave of stunned
horror comes over you as you hear the single word: GUILTY
and find yourself staring in a state of hypnotic trance at the
judge as he puts on the black cap to pronounce sentence of
death – ON YOU !   There remain the dreadful uncertainties
of your last weeks in the condemned cell ; the mounting tension as the inevitable day draws closer; the macabre ritual
of your last meal on earth ; the short procession to the gal-
lows ; death

YOU'VE SEEN IT HAPPEN TO OTHERS – NOW
EXPERIENCE IT FOR YOURSELF !

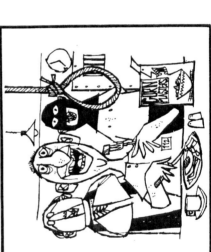

Available exclusively to fully paid up members of the
leisure promotions Experience-of-the Month Club.

New Life

Compilation One: Anatomy of Bewilderment, 2009.
Previously unpublished.

You've given us a rundown here, Mr Herbison, on what might, for want of a better term, be called your life…

That's right.

…and we are, quite frankly, at a bit of a loss to know how to deal with it. We've tried…largely, in your case, I have to admit, for the laughs…to put some of it through the computer, but the brutal truth, which there's no point in my disguising, is that… to be absolutely blunt…it doesn't want to know. Look at it how you will, it's simply not the kind of life there's any real call for. It isn't something that a sophisticated data processing system is prepared to accept for handling.

What's wrong with his life?

It's what I would describe, in broad terms, Mrs Yarmouth, as ramshackle. One gets the impression of something just thrown together at random in an altogether amateurish way with very little thought as to what purpose it was ultimately intended to serve. How it has managed to keep going as a more or less viable entity for as long as it has is frankly something of a mystery.

What would you…?

Where people, as in this case, go wrong is in living their lives in a piecemeal kind of way. Nothing tying in properly with anything else. They make no effort to see their lives as an integrated whole. A beginning, a middle and an end. They live their lives for all the world as though Aristotle had never existed. The only thing I can suggest here is to start the whole thing from scratch all over again and see whether it isn't possible to introduce something resembling order into the chaos. I'm far from sanguine as to the outcome but we have to start somewhere.

This is not what I came here to listen to. When I approached you it was with a view to realising my hidden potential… 'Why be content to remain a big fish in a little pool when the world could be your oyster?'… that was your sales pitch.

That was just an advertisement.

On the strength of which I came to you.

True.

Let's have a look at you, you said. Habits, lifestyle, prejudices, general demeanour, attitudes…and then we'll put the computer to work and see what it comes up with.

What we hoped for hasn't materialised. It's as simple as that, Mr Herbison.

Not just now, thanks

The Lodestone, Birkbeck College, Spring/Summer 1953

★ Write about "YOU" ★
and
■ Increase your income ■

Your "SELF"
can make saleable MSS.

Some people can go out with a spade at the first sign of Spring, dig up one half of a rusty old pair of compasses which got bent being used as a tin-opener three Christmasses before, knock a couple of saleable manuscripts out of it, put it carefully in a box with a tattered copy of an out-of-date guarantee for a different pair of compasses, post it off to the makers for free replacement, muttering something about craftsmanship these days, sit down at their drawing board, and wait. If they want to measure themselves against anything tougher they might do worse than make a start with my 'self' – it's theirs for the asking and I wish them joy of it.

No. The only way – and I've gone into this from practically every angle – the only way this makes sense to me is literally. Because what is a manuscript if it isn't ninety-nine per cent paper? And don't they make paper… Yes. Don't waste time looking it up. They make it out of old bits of chewed-up rag.

Take it any other way and in no time you'll find yourself bogged down in more theories than sanity is likely to stand for. About the least fanciful theory is that there's a misprint. It isn't easy to see how a shelf could make saleable manuscripts, but there's something straight and true and reliable about a good stout shelf, and when you bear in mind that there are two sides to selling anything and that one of them involves buying it, I know which I'd go for. Unless it happened to be the kind that sags in the middle, in which case there might just as well not *be* any misprint.

And anyhow that wouldn't dispose of the bit about increasing your income. If I ever do start succumbing to a lot of Quixotic notions like that, pretty nearly the last thing I shall fall victim to will be any disposition to write about my 'self.' As long as my bank account gets reopened every month with a credit from the public body who are, you might say, paying for my 'self' on extended terms, it is better for everybody that they should remain as far as possible in ignorance about what it is they are laying out good money for. Public money at that. The expression on their face when they do find out will bear comparison I dare say with the expression on the face of the prospective Conservative candidate's wife when she plunges her hand into a bran tub at a Garden Fete and brings it out clutching an autographed figurine of Sir Waldron Smithers.

Even if I did capitulate on the principle of the thing, what is there I could write *about*? I never do anything. Nothing ever happens to me. Each night I set my alarm clock by listening for the click and working the whole thing out from first principles because both the hands have come off, and each morning my day begins with a triumph for empiricism. Moreover I know how to take an insult. Apart from that and glancing over my shoulder every time I go inside a public house on account of a totally abstaining home background in early childhood, you could get my 'self' inside a minus sign. *And* rattle it about.

Think of all the qualities you can make saleable manuscripts out of. Eccentricity, for one. Eccentricity sells like mad – but it just doesn't ever occur to anybody to see anything bizarre in me. Or vice. Vice will fetch a rattling good price in any currency, but you can't stretch vice to include punctuality. No. The more I go rooting about deep down inside my 'self' the more contemptuous I get with what I bring up. I wouldn't pay a man to take it away let alone sell it. I thought at first I might at least bring one manuscript to a head by striking up a kind of shamefaced acquaintance with what in me passes for moral courage. That's what I thought until I took it over to the light and had a good look at it. I must have had it second-hand from the proverbial character who wouldn't say 'Boo' to a goose, because 'Boo' is precisely what I wouldn't say to a goose myself. And that not out of indifference but from policy. I wouldn't say 'Boo' to a duck either as far as that goes. That's what my pluck adds up to. Anybody can capitalise valour and daring, but what can you make of the sort of cringing chicken-heartedness that never failed to send me clambering blindly over an assault course rather than face ignominy like a man? My 'self' in war would only insult the paper it was written on, and the paper it was written on would spit the words back in my face as likely as not.

Socially I never started. As far as other people are concerned I come about as close to a zero of impingement as anybody can this side of death. 'Zero of impingement' is a phrase I once heard from James Thurber over lunch and jotted down afterwards. (Actually I never knew anybody who would think up a phrase like 'zero of impingement' over lunch or any other time, let alone James Thurber. And anyway I always go off with my sandwiches at lunch time. I must have read it somewhere and the only reason I say I heard it from James Thurber over lunch is in case people think I never get out and meet anybody. Whereas of course if there's one thing I never do more than I never do anything else it's get out and meet anybody. I like it better that way.)

And if that's the sort of 'self' they want to have me making saleable manuscripts out of, there's nothing they remind me of so much as a bunch of dispirited film technicians on location in Belfast, hanging about for a chance to shoot the one sequence which doesn't call for wet tramlines. And like a bunch of dispirited film technicians on location in Belfast hanging about for a chance to shoot the one sequence which doesn't call for wet tramlines, they might just as well pack up and go home.

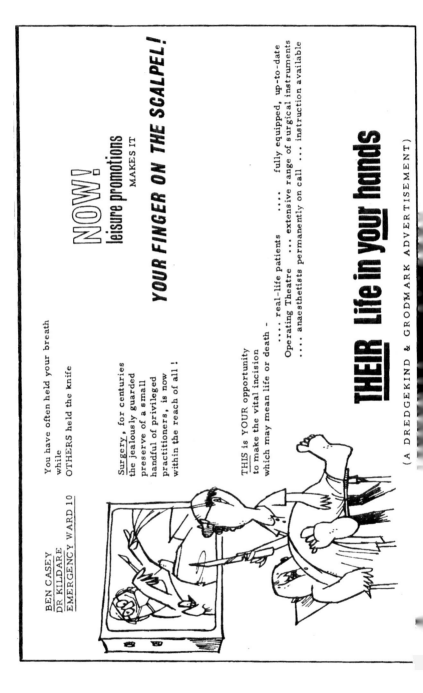

Private Eye #25, 30 November 1962

Nudism

World in Ferment, BBC Two, 23 June 1969

NANCY CHUFF
....
GERALD PIKESTAFF
....

NANCY: We have with us in the studio Gerald Pikestaff, who, as Director of Nudist Studies at the National Garment Manufacturers Research Association, must for professional reasons remain anonymous, but who is very much an authority on the question of contemporary nudism. I would like to ask him to what extent the whole nudist concept is in the melting-pot at the present time.

GERALD: My own feeling, Nancy, is that it's very much so. What we're seeing today is nudism very much on the offensive, and…

NANCY: The London School of Nudism being a case in point.

GERALD: As people try to get on the bandwagon.

NANCY: I believe one of their slogans is 'Complete nudity in six months or money refunded'.

GERALD: It is indeed, Nancy, and I think we're undoubtedly going to see more and more nudists infiltrating themselves into positions of power in the community in the next few years. At present they are lying low, but this is possibly an ominous sign and they may well be biding their time.

NANCY: What kind of places are they secreting themselves in, Gerald, in your experience?

GERALD: Well – we've been looking at grand pianos earlier in the programme. This is one likely spot where a nudist with an eye to the main chance might well secrete himself. A lilo across the wires – it's an open invitation to anyone with nudist leanings, and I should be very surprised indeed if one were to lift the lid of a good many grand pianos and not find one or two individuals in a state of nature inside. Which, of course, provided they have a licence, is perfectly within the law.

NANCY: In other words, you'd advocate padlocks and chains.

GERALD: That would be one answer, Nancy, yes, if the thing's to be really nipped in the bud before it takes hold and spreads from grand pianos to other things, like cocktail cabinets. Because it's no good deluding ourselves that it's going to stop there, and anything less than the most stringent precautions is simply handing the thing over on a plate to the people who want to turn society into a hotbed of rampant nudism in all its shapes and forms.

The Odd Crustacean Won't Come Amiss

Harper's Bazaar, December 1965

MISS TRASIMAN
....
MR BONHOLD
....
MR THICKNEY
....
MR HOSPORT
....

TRASIMAN: Good morning, sir. Can I help you?

BONHOLD: Good morning. I'd like to see the buyer.

TRASIMAN: Yes, sir. I'll get him for you. Mr Thickney! There's a gentleman wanting to see the buyer.

THICKNEY: Oh. Right.

TRASIMAN: Mr Thickney has just gone to find him for you. He won't keep you waiting very long, if you'd care to sit down for a moment.

BONHOLD: Thank you.

Pause.

HOSPORT: Good morning, sir. I'm afraid the buyer has been lured to his death by a vampire bat. Can I help you?

BONHOLD: Help me what?

HOSPORT: I understood you were in a drugged stupor and looking for a clockwork hummingbird, sir.

BONHOLD: No. I wasn't.

HOSPORT: In that case we seem to be somewhat at cross purposes, sir. What can I show you?

BONHOLD: I'd like to see the seating arrangements for the Lord Mayor's Banquet, if it's not too much trouble.

HOSPORT: Certainly, sir. Mr Thickney! Show this gentleman a tray of rings and brooches, will you?

THICKNEY: Yes, Mr Hosport.

HOSPORT: Perhaps you'd care to make a selection from these.

BONHOLD: Thank you.

THICKNEY: You'll find those go very nicely with a bunch of grapes, sir.

BONHOLD: Aha.

THICKNEY: Or a tin and a half of condensed milk.

BONHOLD: Do you happen to have anything in the way of a bunch of grapes? That I could see them against.

THICKNEY: No, sir. I don't think we do. I rather think that the nearest I could find to a bunch of grapes in the shop at the moment would be this pair of old meat skewers.

BONHOLD: Yes. I see.

THICKNEY: Very useful, of course. For high days and holidays.

BONHOLD: Yes.

THICKNEY: Or if it turned out to be a pair you'd got already, you could always bring them back and we'd exchange them for a secondhand spiral staircase.

BONHOLD: No. I don't think so.

THICKNEY: This is rather novel, sir.

BONHOLD: What is it? A brooch of some kind?

THICKNEY: That's right, sir.

BONHOLD: Strange shape.

THICKNEY: It is rather quaint, sir, isn't it? Part of a frogman's kneecap.

BONHOLD: Ah, yes. Taken at the moment of impact, I imagine.

THICKNEY: Very shortly after, yes, sir.

BONHOLD: Some of the original paintwork still visible, I see.

THICKNEY: Oh yes. It's quite authentic.

BONHOLD: Very nice. What I'm really looking for, if you have such a thing, is a present for my wife's sister's second cousin.

THICKNEY: Ah.

BONHOLD: Damn young fool's got himself shipped off to Hong Kong in a boat bound for Venezuela.

THICKNEY: And landed up in Zanzibar, I expect. It's what usually happens in that sort of situation, don't you find, sir?

BONHOLD: Left from Tilbury three or four minutes ago, the young tartar. I can't have missed him by more than a couple of days.

THICKNEY: It's often the way things are, sir.

BONHOLD: Spoke to someone in a blue serge suit on the quayside just before he went on board. Said he was off on safari and could he leave a message.

THICKNEY: Thank heaven for that, then, sir.

BONHOLD: He'll be in mid-Atlantic by now. Unless I'm very much mistaken. Taking pot-shots. It's always been one of his ambitions.

THICKNEY: Really, sir?

BONHOLD: Oh, yes. He used to talk about it when he was a toddler. 'It's the big stuff I'm really after,' he used to say, 'but the odd crustacean won't come amiss.'

THICKNEY: Many a true word, sir.

BONHOLD: He tried it out once. On a raft.

THICKNEY: In mid-Atlantic, sir?

BONHOLD: Yes. That's what *we* said. But he wouldn't listen.

THICKNEY: It sounds a mite chancy, sir.

BONHOLD: We went out to him. In a towing boat. Try and get him to see reason. But we might have saved ourselves the trouble.

THICKNEY: No go, sir?

BONHOLD: 'What happens if you capsize,' we said. But no, he wouldn't have it. 'Unsinkable,' he said. 'That's what I am on this raft.'

THICKNEY: Foolish.

BONHOLD: 'You can keep all your Titanics,' he said. 'Every single man jack of them. They're not worth the water they float on.'

THICKNEY: There's only *been* one Titanic, surely.

BONHOLD: 'Yes,' he said. 'And that sank.'

THICKNEY: Well, well.

BONHOLD: So of course there was nothing for it but to row back.

THICKNEY: Naturally.

BONHOLD: Not, mind you, that I can see it lasting.

THICKNEY: No?

BONHOLD: Went off to the Arctic not so long ago. Set off full of ideas and a boatload of immersion heaters – he was back inside six months. In a considerably chastened mood.

THICKNEY: Really?

BONHOLD: Reckoned to have seen giraffe up there.

THICKNEY: In the Arctic?

BONHOLD: Whole colony of them. On an iceberg.

THICKNEY: Good God!

BONHOLD: All completely nude, of course.

THICKNEY: Yes?

BONHOLD: Not that he'd notice – he wasn't that sort. But I suppose giraffes on an iceberg, so why not big game in mid-Atlantic? You can see how his mind must have been working.

THICKNEY: How did they get there?

BONHOLD: The giraffes? Goodness only knows. I dare say they felt entitled to ask him the same question. What of course he thinks he can do. Single-handed. He'll need beaters, he'll need ghillies, he'll need staghounds. It's madness.

THICKNEY: Someone should have warned him, sir.

BONHOLD: We did. We told him. He said he'd cross that hurdle when he came to it. Admittedly he's got an elephant gun, but as I said to him, it takes an elephant to handle one of those.

THICKNEY: Personally I should have thought a harpoon was more in keeping.

BONHOLD: What he imagines he's going to find, with one or without.

THICKNEY: He might hit on a whale, if he's lucky, but I can't frankly see much likelihood of zebra.

BONHOLD: I got the impression he was thinking more in terms of bison.

THICKNEY: Even so, sir.

BONHOLD: Quite.

THICKNEY: So now I suppose it's a question of finding something to remind him of the District Attorney's office in Nashville, Tennessee?

BONHOLD: It is. Yes. That or something as near to it as one can get.

THICKNEY: Such as the disused marshalling yard, perhaps? Behind the Scunthorpe and District Dyeworks in Lower Parsifal Street.

BONHOLD: That *type* of thing.

THICKNEY: In that case, might I suggest the Eiffel Tower, sir?

BONHOLD: Ah.

THICKNEY: There's a restaurant at the top. And several hundred thousand rivets holding the thing together. It might be just what he's looking for.

BONHOLD: It might, indeed. Whether or not he'll find it, of course, is another matter. His eyesight isn't all it might be.

THICKNEY: Oh. I'm sorry to hear that, sir. Perhaps it might be an idea to give him an eye-test, in that case? Or if you preferred, we could give him one for you.

BONHOLD: You could?

THICKNEY: Oh, yes, sir. Nothing easier.

BONHOLD: How long would it take?

THICKNEY: By air mail? About six and a half days. At this time of the year.

BONHOLD: I see.

THICKNEY: Would you care to see what we've got? In the way of sight-testing cards.

BONHOLD: Yes. I think perhaps I would.

THICKNEY: We don't stock a wide range, but we have these two. There's this one, which you can hang up on a wall and read off at twenty-eight yards. Or there's this identical one, which can be stood on a flat surface somewhere, and read off in exactly the same manner at either ten feet or thirty-three yards, whichever is the more convenient.

BONHOLD: I see. Yes. Well, supposing I settle for this one.

THICKNEY: Certainly, sir. I'll wrap it up for you.

BONHOLD: How much is it?

THICKNEY: Ninety-three pounds and four-pence, sir.

BONHOLD: Right.

THICKNEY: I'll just put a protective covering round it first, front and back, so that it doesn't get damaged by the brown paper.

BONHOLD: What is it? As a matter of interest. That you're putting round it.

THICKNEY: It's a laminated material, which prevents indentations appearing on the surface through contact with outside agencies.

BONHOLD: Ah.

THICKNEY: There. Now we can use ordinary wrapping paper on it without fear of anything coming off on the underside.

BONHOLD: Excellent.

THICKNEY: I don't know whether you've tried reading one of these eye-testing cards through a megaphone, at any time, sir?

BONHOLD: No. I can't say I have.

THICKNEY: One or two customers have had some very pleasing results that way, sir.

BONHOLD: A bit hard on the neighbours, isn't it?

THICKNEY: They seem to thrive on it, sir, strangely enough. There, sir. And if it should give any trouble, just drop it in and we'll overhaul it free of charge. But I don't think it will. There's a five-year guarantee.

BONHOLD: Thank you very much.

THICKNEY: Not at all, sir. A pleasure. And I hope your friend manages to find his way back from Venezuala without too much trouble.

BONHOLD: I expect he will. If he doesn't, we'll have to ship him off to Hong Kong and let him sort it out for himself.

THICKNEY: Quite, sir.

BONHOLD: That's the only answer to that one. And trust to luck he doesn't finish up in Zanzibar.

THICKNEY: Ah – well. That's one of the imponderables, sir, isn't it?

BONHOLD: It certainly is.

THICKNEY: Goodbye, sir.

BONHOLD: Goodbye.

HOSPORT: Mr Thickney.

THICKNEY: Yes, Mr Hosport.

HOSPORT: Another time you get a customer like that, refer him to me, will you?

THICKNEY: Yes, Mr Hosport.

HOSPORT: There's no need for you cope on your own.

THICKNEY: No, Mr Hosport.

Oh

The Queen, 8 June 1960

HUMPHREY SAVERNAKE
LAURA SAVERNAKE

HUMPHREY: No, Laura, I don't think it's the kind of thing we could expect Graham to show much interest in.

LAURA: Oh?

HUMPHREY: He's very orthodox in many ways. As far as his painting is concerned.

LAURA: I must say he doesn't show much preference for orthodox methods in anything else.

HUMPHREY: All the same, Laura, I think that to fix the brush in a vice and move the canvas about on the end of it would create more problems than it would solve.

LAURA: I should have thought it would have been the very thing for Graham.

HUMPHREY: I'll suggest it to him, of course – but you mustn't be surprised if he turns it down. Don't forget he's got all this fuss on his mind still about Colonel Padlock's portrait – that must be taking up practically every spare minute of his time.

LAURA: What fuss about Colonel Padlock's portrait? He's finished it. He *must* have.

HUMPHREY: He's had a great deal to do, Laura.

LAURA: You don't mean to say poor Colonel Padlock is still sitting there? Waiting?

HUMPHREY: It isn't just a matter of setting an easel up, Laura, and a canvas, and beginning to paint. Just like that.

LAURA: I think that's absolutely disgraceful! What for heaven's sake has he been doing?

HUMPHREY: He hasn't been wasting his time, my dear.

LAURA: Six weeks it must be since all this started. At least. I can't think what he can have been doing all that time.

HUMPHREY: So far as I know, Colonel Padlock hasn't complained.

LAURA: Why on earth doesn't he get people to help him?

HUMPHREY: You won't persuade Graham to delegate responsibility, my dear.

LAURA: Doing every single thing himself from scratch.

HUMPHREY: Yes, well, there it is. If he prefers to work that way…

LAURA: I'd say nothing if it were simply a question of constructing his own easels. With homemade glue.

HUMPHREY: After all…

LAURA: Or even weaving his canvases himself. But growing his own hemp or whatever it is to do it with! That's carrying it too far.

HUMPHREY: Yes, well – I'm afraid I side with Graham over this, Laura.

LAURA: Felling the timber himself for his brush handles and planing it down till it's small enough.

HUMPHREY: What other way is there, Laura, if you're determined to keep control over the finished picture? And that's the whole crux of it as far as Graham is concerned. As you know.

LAURA: And in the meantime, Colonel Padlock has to sit there.

HUMPHREY: As far as that goes, I should think Colonel Padlock would be the last person to want to see Graham compromise his professional integrity on his account.

LAURA: So he just has to sit waiting. While Graham goes off all over the world looking for natural pigments and one thing and another.

HUMPHREY: My dear Laura, what else can he possibly do but collect the pigments? He can't paint without them. Be sensible.

LAURA: No. *(Quietly and unemphatically after a brief pause.)* But there's an artist's colourman not three doors away.

HUMPHREY: You don't seem to understand, Laura.

LAURA: And I can't see how it could possibly hurt his professional integrity to at least buy his brushes ready-made.

HUMPHREY: Perhaps not, but…

LAURA: A whole Sunday morning spent going over one camel for the sake of three or four miserable hairs! It's utterly ridiculous!

HUMPHREY: In any case, that part of it's more or less finished. It's this wretched problem now of where to sit Colonel Padlock. How far back from the easel.

LAURA: *(After a shocked pause.)* That was decided.

HUMPHREY: Not finally, my dear.

LAURA: It really is too bad!

HUMPHREY: Yes, well…

LAURA: How many months is it since we all sat round listening to Graham explaining about 'giving the background a chance' and 'not letting the sitter choke the canvas' and all the rest of it?

HUMPHREY: It's one thing to have worked something out in principle, Laura. It's a different matter putting it into practice.

LAURA: All he has to do surely is to sit Colonel Padlock far enough back from the easel. That shouldn't take him eight weeks.

HUMPHREY: Don't forget Colonel Padlock is travelling backwards. It's bound to slow him down a little bit.

LAURA: *Travelling* backwards?

HUMPHREY: You know Graham as well as I do, my dear. He doesn't often do things by halves.

Pause.

LAURA: That, I suppose, accounts for his sending home for field-glasses.

HUMPHREY: It's gone well beyond field-glasses, Laura.

LAURA: Oh? What is it now, then? Descriptions once a week by transatlantic telephone?

HUMPHREY: Every half hour, actually. By ticker tape.

LAURA: *(Weakly.)* I see.

HUMPHREY: Or that was the position at any rate last week. He was in Yokohama then.

LAURA: Who was in Yokohama?

HUMPHREY: Colonel Padlock. *(Pause.)* He's in all probability more than halfway round the globe by now.

LAURA: Oh. *(Pause.)* What happens when he's circled it?

HUMPHREY: They're expecting to end up back to back.

LAURA: Back to *what*?

HUMPHREY: That's if Graham's calculations are as reliable as he thinks they are.

   Pause.

LAURA: I see.

HUMPHREY: And by that time he hopes to have the television cameras ready. *(Pause.)* Rigged up behind him. *(Pause.)* And if he puts the screen where he can get a clear view of it while he's painting, he can go right ahead the moment Colonel Padlock comes in range of the cameras. *(Pause.)* I think it rather appeals to Graham – the idea of painting direct from a television screen. *(Pause.)* It would, of course.

   Long pause.

LAURA: I suppose as soon as he gets back we ought to send him a greetings telegram.

HUMPHREY: Who?

LAURA: Colonel Padlock. If he ever does.

   Pause.

HUMPHREY: I suppose we ought.

   Curtain.

Memo:

<u>Due in Galashiels on Tuesday week!</u>

                            Uncle once. Uncle by marriage. Due
                            in Galashiels on Thursday fortnight.

Roger's cousin, come to that. Due in Galashiels three
weeks come Michaelmas.

                            Look at Doris's sister, then. Due in
                            Galashiels a week on Friday ever since she
                            was kneehigh to a grasshopper.

(And yet, when you come down to it, there must be a
whole host of people who've gone through their entire
lives without ever having been due in Galashiels at all!)

                                    It's a strange old world

Compilation One: Anatomy of Bewilderment, 2009. Previously unpublished.

Oh, this grinding comfort!

The Tribune, 17 April 1953.
N.F. Simpson's earliest known professional writing.

One result of increasing the judges' salaries would be, according to some Government supporters, 'to expose to the general public the severity with which present tax rates fall on the higher salaries.' So said *The Times* of March 24th.

Another thing that could well do with being exposed to the general public is the ruinous expense involved in living up to these higher salaries. And if the general public all read *The Times* every morning, this jolly well would have been exposed.

The first thing they would have no excuse for not knowing, is that the vast moral authority of the law is bound up with 'the visible dignity of the men who dispense the Queen's justice.' The general public – ninnies! – are quite capable of thinking that 'visible dignity' begins and ends with a snugly fitting wig.

How different is the real story. This has been brought home to me in the last few weeks by letter after heartbreaking letter in *The Times*. 'The expenses that have to be met, the standards which have to be maintained.' The words are those of Sir Hartley Shawcross, but the grim and harrowing facts behind them are the daily experience of the men who dispense the Queen's justice.

Try to picture the standards these men are obliged to maintain day in, day out, in the pursuit of their calling: the awful repletion of it, the leisure, the grinding comfort. It is little enough to ask, surely, that they should not also be left alone to bear the cost of it.

The situation must be infinitely worse for eminent people in industry, commerce and the other professions, many of whom, we read, are being virtually crippled financially by the standards which have to be maintained on even higher salaries.

We hear a lot about old age pensioners being unable to make a pound or two working part-time, because whatever they get that way puts paid to their pension. They ought to be thankful.

Listen to this, from a poignant letter which appeared in *The Times* only last week: 'If the man, or his wife, happens to have a considerable private income, the position is still worse, and it is impossible to pay him any worthwhile net income for working, however valuable his services may be – a means test if ever there was one.'

Here is the kind of human problem which must always take its most acute form amongst the over-privileged; but even amongst the general public it is by no means unknown for an income from one source to cancel out an income from another. I am thinking more particularly of those who are deprived of all unemployment benefit whatsoever, for no other reason than that they are getting paid for working at some job or other.

The world is full of injustices of this kind. Several people personally known to me are finding it impossible to draw public assistance because they happen to be earning a good salary already.

And what is this precious Government of ours doing about it? You might think they would at least try to ease the burden of the higher income groups by bringing them more into line with the general public, who are enjoying the comparative leniency with which present tax rates fall on the smaller salaries.

But what in fact *are* they doing? Believe it or not, they are – callously and with total disregard for human suffering – planning to burden our hard-hit judiciary with yet another thousand a year. Which end of which wedge this will turn out to be, I am still far too confused to be able to say on the spur of the moment.

N.F. SIMPSON

On Teeth

Snippets Two, BBC Radio 3, 17 March 1983. Revised 2006.

Hereward the Wake's teeth were a byword. Indeed, it was in
a moment of exasperation that he had them out. True, he had
them replaced with dentures, but they were a bad fit and had
a habit of slipping forward. It was embarrassing. People had to
look away. Once, indeed, when he was addressing his troops on
the eve of a battle, they came right out and had to be shoved back
in again. The charisma goes when this kind of thing happens,
and it is not always possible in these circumstances to retain the
allegiance of one's men. In some ways it can be looked upon
as the acid test of leadership. If you can retain the confidence
of your men in spite of having your teeth slip forward every
time you utter a word of command – blurring your speech and
leaving your troops in doubt as to what the command actually
is – you are a born leader of men and may safely say so on
application forms. It's when they come out altogether that it
becomes a serious problem. During a battle. And get trodden
in. It has always been a bone of contention amongst historians
to what extent you can say goodbye to a set of dentures that
falls out on the battlefield, and to what extent it's possible to
retrieve them if you saw where they went. Even then, you were
up against the problem of knowing whether they were yours
or somebody else's. One set of dentures looks very much like
another when it's covered in mud. The proof of the pudding,
one imagines, was in the eating, so to speak. You put them in,
and if, mud notwithstanding, they fitted, the likelihood was
that they were yours. Or would do until yours turned up. Mud,
though, was one thing, sand another. During the Crusades, it
was getting a mouthful of sand and grit whenever one tried a set
of dentures for size that was the bugbear. It must have given a
slight balance of advantage to the Saracens, for whom it was by
way of being an occupational hazard with which they had long
since learned to cope. They did so by having their dentures
fastened on with elastic, so that should they shoot out during a
particularly fierce encounter, they would bob up and down and
not fall into the sand. There were drawbacks, in that, during
the course of a more than usually vigorous engagement, they

could shoot out and then fly back in your face, catching you between the eyes and momentarily blinding you. Suleiman the Magnificent, indeed, got his dentures wound round his ear in some peculiar way when something he was eating went down the wrong way, but this was an eventuality that, as a Saracen, you had to learn to live with. Dentistry, it goes without saying, has come a long way since then. The golden rule, it seems to me, when having dentures fitted, is to insist on sobriety in the dentist you have taken your custom to. An inebriated dentist has rarely been a wholly satisfactory dentist. Unless he can stand up unassisted, give him a wide berth. And never, under any circumstances, allow a dentist, inebriated or not, into an attic. I remember vividly having to throw one out from an attic. Bodily. Through the window. And his chair after him. It will be objected, by the puritanically minded, that this is an anti-social act. It's all very well, one can hear them argue, to have a dentist come flying out of an upstairs window, but that you take the full brunt if you happen to be standing underneath. This is true, and hard to answer. Asking the average dentist in this situation to take evasive action is woefully unrealistic, since, by landing on a passerby, he can reasonably expect to knock out one or two teeth, and taking your chances when they come is what dentistry is all about. This sounds like opportunism, but one must try to see it from the dentist's point of view: two teeth here, three teeth there – it all adds up. Indeed, a heavily built dentist who has been taught how to fall should be able to account for a good many more teeth if he chooses his moment with any sort of flair. It's largely a question of how you land. There is a knack. You have it, or you don't have it, but training can bring out what's there. An interesting thought, in this connection, is that it cannot be entirely coincidental that so many of the dentists one meets, in the street or socially, as well as in the course of their professional duty, are shaped like boomerangs. And yet a moment's thought should suffice to explain why. For if you are born shaped like a wee boomerang, it is a pretty clear indication that nature has singled you out for a dental career, and wise parents, recognising this, will take care to steer you towards dentistry, knowing that you will have the edge over other less fortunate colleagues when it comes to returning to base through the window you came out of in order to retrieve your overalls without disturbing the people downstairs. And yet, all this having been said, it is well to bear in mind that there is quite a respectable body of reputable practitioners who have got through their entire careers without having been thrown out of an upstairs window at all.

How far would you go along with this as a description of yourself?

Well…

As far as Woking…?

Only if I were going that way.

Compilation One: Anatomy of Bewilderment, 2009. Previously unpublished.

One Blast and Have Done

The Queen, 28 September 1960

FREDA

IVY

FREDA: Ivy!

IVY: Hallo, Freda.

FREDA: Come in. Sit down and have a cup of tea.

IVY: No, thank you, Freda. I mustn't stop. I'm on the cadge really. You wouldn't have such a thing as a flute? We've had a flautist call.

FREDA: A flute. Goodness.

IVY: No warning or anything.

FREDA: I'm just trying to think, Ivy. I know we did have one.

IVY: We haven't got a thing in the house except percussion.

FREDA: I suppose a bassoon wouldn't do? If I can find one.

IVY: Anything at all, Freda.

FREDA: I'll see what there is in the cupboard.

IVY: As long as it's something he can blow down.

FREDA: He wants to be able to blow across it, really, if he's a flautist but…no, there's only this. Would that do, do you think? It's one of mum's old bassoons. She never uses it.

IVY: That would do fine, Freda.

FREDA: I think it works all right. As long as he doesn't mind a bit of coal dust in it.

IVY: If you're sure you can spare it.

FREDA: Let me put a duster over it for you. Get some of the worst off.

IVY: Don't bother, Freda.

FREDA: It won't take a minute.

IVY: He could have made do with it as it was.

FREDA: I wish I knew where to put my hands on a flute for you. There's one somewhere I'm almost certain. We had an old harmonium with a flute in it at one time but I don't know till Tom gets in what he's done with it.

IVY: It doesn't matter, Freda. This is fine.

FREDA: Tell him to mind the coal dust inside when he starts to blow.

IVY: It gets into everything, doesn't it?

FREDA: We had *coal* once.

IVY: No!

FREDA: We did. In the American organ. Great lumps the size of cricket balls.

IVY: How on earth did that happen?

FREDA: We made the mistake of lending it to some people we knew down the road. And that's how it came back.

IVY: With coal in it.

FREDA: And all stuck in any old how, of course. At the back and underneath.

IVY: It's not right, is it?

FREDA: No attempt at putting all the big lumps together, or separating out the slack, or anything like that.

IVY: Too much trouble.

FREDA: Under the bellows and everywhere. I said to Tom – you'll never play it while it's in that state.

IVY: It's not the place for it.

FREDA: He had a rousing tune he could have played if it hadn't been for that. Nearly a hundredweight of it altogether there must have been when we cleared it out.

IVY: Fancy.

FREDA: What's that noise?

IVY: I didn't hear anything.

FREDA: I thought I heard knocking.

Knocks are heard on wall.

IVY: You're right. He's getting impatient for his flute.

FREDA: Who is it? If it's not a rude question.

IVY: I've never set eyes on him before, Freda, in my life. Just came in, out of the blue, about half an hour ago.

FREDA: You haven't left him in there by himself?

IVY: Yes – I'd better go back. Before he starts getting up to anything. This is the second one we've had this week.

FREDA: Go on?

IVY: We had one in on Monday. They seem to be making a bee-line for us for some reason.

FREDA: And what did *he* want?

IVY: Could he come in for a minute and beat hell out of our timpani, if you please!

FREDA: No!

IVY: No credentials or anything, of course.

FREDA: Isn't it the limit?

IVY: Tried to tell me he was over here on a day trip from Vladivostok.

FREDA: *That* speaks volumes.

IVY: Looking for his brother.

FREDA: Just as well it was a Monday.

IVY: In any case, even if he was genuine, you don't want complete strangers walking in whenever they feel like it and going for all they're worth at your timpani.

FREDA: Of course you don't. *(Knocking repeated.)* There he is again. He's getting impatient.

IVY: *(Shouts.)* I'm just coming. *(To FREDA.)* If it had been anything but timpani I should very likely have fallen for it, but it so happened I was saving the timpani for Fred and Doris when they came in, so they could have a bit of percussion before they went to bed. Otherwise I might have let him in.

Knocking repeated.

FREDA: You'll have him singing in there, Ivy. All over the furniture.

IVY: *(Going.)* Goodness – don't say that. I don't want that happening. I've had enough singing to last *me* for a little while. I didn't tell you about Wednesday, did I?

FREDA: Not Mrs Bargold again?

IVY: *(Returning.)* You know what a nice afternoon it was, Wednesday – after it brightened up. So I thought I'll just have half an hour with a book out in the garden while I can…

FREDA: And Mrs Bargold started up.

IVY: Started up! I've never heard anything like it. Right through the trellis-work.

FREDA: It isn't as if she's exactly a Peach Melba, either.

IVY: I stuck it for as long as I could, but…

FREDA: She must have a sixth sense.

IVY: Every time I sit down out there. In the end I called over to her. I couldn't stand it any longer. I said I don't mind you singing, Mrs Bargold – but not through my trellis-work if you don't mind.

FREDA: It's not as if it's just once or twice, is it?

IVY: 'Rock of Ages'. Full blast at the top of her voice.

FREDA: 'Rock of Ages'? That's a change, isn't it?

IVY: Right through the trellis-work. I couldn't read or do anything.

FREDA: I don't think I've heard Mrs Bargold sing 'Rock of Ages' since Mr Stepupper called her in to sing down the overflow pipe while the stopcock was being seen to.

IVY: I told her – I didn't have trellis-work put up for her to sing 'Rock of Ages' through whenever it happened to suit her convenience.

FREDA: Of course not.

IVY: It's not cheap, either. Ten-and-six a yard it was, all told, to put up. With the labour.

FREDA: I can imagine.

IVY: I complained about the nails too. Thick green mould all over them where she's been corroding them month in month out.

FREDA: It's no joke getting it off, either. Especially on her side of the fence.

IVY: I have to stand on a step-ladder and lean right over. I wouldn't mind so much if it was ordinary rust. You'd get that with anything. You'd get it with the National Anthem. But this isn't rust – it's green mould. She must be able to see it forming in front of her eyes, but she makes no attempt to stop.

FREDA: The same as what Mrs Bates had, I expect. On her front door. It took her nearly a week to get it off. Somebody singing 'Shenandoah' through her letter-box when she was out.

IVY: And do you know what she had the cheek to say to me? She said I was the first one who'd complained! *(Mimicking.)* 'No one else has ever complained.'

FREDA: Only because they knew it wouldn't make any difference.

IVY: I told her – I wouldn't have minded so much if they'd been stainless steel.

FREDA: Or plastic.

IVY: 'No one else has complained!' I said to her – no one else has had 'Rock of Ages' sung through their trellis-work week after week for months on end.

A single, prolonged, loud note from a trombone is heard.

IVY: What was that?

FREDA: It sounded like a trombone, Ivy.

IVY: *(Going off.)* What's he getting up to in there?

FREDA: *(Loudly, after her.)* He couldn't wait, I expect. He's blown down the nearest thing. *(Pause. Then in an undertone, sardonically.)* 'Nothing in the house except percussion!'

Curtain.

One of our St Bernard Dogs is Missing

Closedown, BBC Two, 21 February 1977. Later published in *A Way with Words* (Sinclair Browne, 1982)

A moot point
Whether I was going to
Make it.
I just had the strength
To ring the bell.

There were monks inside
And one of them
Eventually
Opened the door.
Oh
He said,
This is a bit of a turn-up
He said
For the book.
Opportune
He said
Your arriving at this particular
As it were
Moment

You're dead right
I said
It was touch and go
Whether I could have managed
To keep going
For very much
Longer.

No
He said
The reason I used the word opportune
Is that
Not to put too fine a point on it

One of our St Bernard dogs is
Unfortunately
Missing.

Oh, dear
I said.
Not looking for me, I hope.

No
He said.
It went for a walk
And got lost in the snow.

Dreadful thing
I said
To happen.

Yes
He said.
It is.

To
Of all creatures
I said
A St Bernard dog
That has devoted
Its entire
Life
To doing good
And helping
Others.

What I was actually thinking
He said
Since you happen to be
In a manner of speaking
Out there already
Is that
If you could
At all
See your way clear
To having a scout

N.F. SIMPSON

As it were
Around,
It would save one of us
Having to
If I can so put it
Turn out.
Ah
I said
That would
I suppose
Make a kind of sense.

Before you go
He said
If I can find it
You'd better
Here it is
Take this.

What is it?
I said
It's a flask
He said
Of brandy.
Ah
I said.

For the dog
He said.

Good thinking
I said.

The drill
He said
When you find it
If you ever do
Is to lie down.

Right
I said
Will do.

Lie down on top of it
He said
To keep it warm
Till help arrives.

That was a week ago and my hopes are rising all the time.
I feel with ever-increasing confidence
that once I can safely say that I am within what might
be called striking distance of knowing where, within a
square mile or two, to start getting down to looking,
my troubles are more or less, to all intents and
purposes, apart from frostbite, with any luck once
help arrives at long last, God willing, as good as over.
It is good to be spurred on with hope.

It has been put to me that some of you, having bought this book in ill-advised haste, may be looking at one another in some dismay after glancing quickly through it, and anxiously canvassing one another's views as to whether or not it looks like being remotely worth what you have paid out good money for. The consensus seems to be that it is for me, as its author, to address these concerns. How best can I do so? Let me put it this way. It's worth it to me. In itself a comforting thought. If, nevertheless, it should turn out to be a wholly different story for you, you will just have to try and be philosophical about it. These things after all happen. It's the way the cookie crumbles. What we gain on the swings we lose on the roundabouts. Life is like that, and there is frankly very little to be done about it. It is only fair to add that if, unwisely in my view, some of you were thinking of asking for your money back, it has, so far as I personally am concerned, already gone. (Knick-knacks. This and that. You know how it is.) Best by far simply to give a wry smile, shrug your shoulders and look on it as a salutary lesson for the future.

Compilation One: Anatomy of Bewilderment, 2009. Previously unpublished.

The Overcoat

Man About Town, December 1960

It was the kind of coat uncle wore and I was pleased to have it. The sleeves were too long but what did that matter? Seven or eight inches meant little to me in those days, and as time has gone on they have come to mean less and less. There were trousers attached to it and this of course was a great innovation at that time, when trousers were very much a separate entity altogether – as indeed they are now – but although I have had the coat for nearly twenty-eight years, and have worn it almost continuously the whole time, the trousers are as much an innovation as ever. Age does not seem in any way to wither them in spite of changing fashions. Another innovation, which we all thought very wonderful at the time, although it would no doubt be taken for granted if it occurred now, was the spare pair of trousers let into the lining at the back ready for any unforeseen emergency. I have never had occasion to use them, though many's the time I have had reason to be grateful for the reassuring feeling that the presence of that 'spare pair', as we called them, gave me. It was this feeling of confidence – the knowledge that if anything untoward were to happen when I was miles from anywhere I should have my old faithfuls to fall back upon – that helped me through many a tight corner. And I still always carry a small pair of scissors about with me 'just in case'.

One of the things which attracted me to the coat immediately I saw it was the fur collar, which unfortunately is no longer attached to it. It came off one day when I was in Bursledown Quarry looking for a ledge wide enough to rest my skates on for a moment or two, while I had a round – if this is the correct word – of bagatelle for old time's sake with a former school friend Blaxon, who was there in the same quarry drying out an old sheepskin rug. So concerned was I about the safety of my skates that my bagatelle must have suffered; at all events I was handsomely defeated. But I did find my skates waiting for me where I had left them, and for this I would have been prepared to put up with any number of defeats. For these were by way of being a somewhat unique pair and I valued them accordingly. One was an ice-skate, one was a roller-skate, and so they were in a sense amphibious – at any rate as a pair, if not individually – for they could be used on both land and water simultaneously, and frequently were. On my walks (if 'walks' is quite the right word), whenever these took me along the bank of a pond or lake in mid-winter, I would proceed with one roller-skated foot on the land, one ice-skated foot on the frozen water. It may not have been the only way to travel, and indeed I am inclined to think on looking back on it now that it was in all probability very far from being so – but my goodness it was *a* way, and in those days what more could one want?

But I am digressing. To return to the overcoat. I was sorry to lose the fur collar (and although I went back afterwards to look for it I never found the slightest trace of it). I was the more sorry because it happened to be one of the few remaining fur collars in England with a genuine secret panel. It may well have been this which attracted the thief or thieves – if such they were – to it, though what hope they could have had of disposing of it, either in the quarry or outside, is to say the least of it a somewhat moot question. Be that as it may, disposed of it they have.

Any secret panel is bound to become the subject of numerous stories, even though it may not have been so to begin with. This one was no exception. Some were undoubtedly authentic, others not so authentic. Charles II, and there may be some truth in this, was said to have hidden behind it on his way to Brighton in 1651 (or Brighthelmstone, as I believe was then called). It was certainly used later on by smugglers and would-be smugglers for concealing whisky and rum from the ever vigilant exciseman. An ideal spot it must have been, too. What customs official, whether in uniform or not, would ever have thought of looking in there? And again in the last war it came into service for the last time as a temporary storehouse for Rembrandts from Inverary. (There were plans, if there had been a landing of German troops, to blow it up with high explosive, together with its contents. So I, as the wearer of the coat, had a rather special reason for wishing Hitler and all his works to the devil!)

Every possible contingency, remote or otherwise, had been provided for. One of the pockets had even been put in the other way up against the possibility that in a moment of absentmindedness one had got into the coat upside down. The buttons too incorporated a device I have never seen anywhere since, though I have often looked out for it. Most buttons are sewn to the fabric with cotton or thread, and once on, there they stay until the thread wears out. If the buttonhole happens to turn up exactly opposite the button – as it frequently does – all is well. The button simply passes through the buttonhole and the garment is fastened. But what of the case – once in perhaps three or four million times – when the buttonhole, through some slight variation in the angle at which one is wearing the coat, is some three or four inches to one side of the button for which it is designed? Or an inch or two above or below it? This is where the special device comes into play, for these buttons are sewn on not with thread but with very strong, very fine elastic, which allows of the greatest possible mobility without the sacrifice of steadiness. The button can be diverted at a moment's notice to any reasonably adjacent point, in order to effect a rendezvous with the buttonhole, and the coat – no matter at what angle the wearer may at any given moment find himself wearing it – need never remain in any real sense unfastened.

I have tried to keep the coat in all respects as it was when it first came into my hands, and in spite of minor setbacks and difficulties this by and large is what I have succeeded in doing. The big patch over the balloon attachment is a poignant reminder of the day I was very nearly buried alive. I was an undergraduate at the time and, as young men will, conceived the wildly harebrained scheme of impersonating a corpse. It so happened however that a funeral was going on nearby at the same time, and as luck would have it one of the undertakers happened to catch sight of me. He called the others across to look at me and in no time at all – they were Italians – a heated controversy had ensued as to which of us was in fact the dead man. Nor was the argument of merely academic interest, since it would have reflected disastrously on their professional expertise to leave a genuine corpse unburied, even by mistake – especially if in the process a man who was alive and in full possession of his faculties were to be interred in his place. It was to avoid such an awkward eventuality that some of the more vocal among them put forward the suggestion – which gained ground far too quickly for my comfort! – that they should bury us both.

And this might well have been the outcome had I not, just in time, remembered the balloon attachment which a thoughtful tailor had incorporated – against, I have not the slightest doubt, just such a contingency as this. I had never had recourse to it before, but I knew something about the basic principle on which the balloon works, and started blowing. I blew as if my life depended on it – as indeed it did. I don't know what the college authorities in solemn state assembled must have made of it. But it undoubtedly saved my life. There was a high-ish wind, and I came down – very much less corpse-like than I had gone up, I may say – in Shropshire, that lovely county. The attachment itself got slightly damaged in the process and I had to have it patched up in the nearest colour to red that was then obtainable – a sort of duck egg blue. I have had it replaced several times since, but the colour for some reason has always remained the same.

So there it is. The only coat of its size in the United Kingdom with an *outside* fire escape. This was put in shortly before it came into my hands by a wealthy eccentric (who used it for getting *into* the coat, oddly enough). I have never had to use it, of course, and I hope I never shall, but it's always good to know it's there. I give it a coat of paint every two or three years. It was the same eccentric owner who was responsible for the flagpole. I have never bothered to take it down, although it is, I believe, detachable; nor have I ever flown a flag from it – except on VE Day and once at half-mast when my son was born. People often mistake it for a periscope – and on a calm day the resemblance is certainly uncanny. I have been put down on more than one occasion as a submarine (and suffered ostracism) on account of it. One of these days I shall probably have it made into something less likely to be misconstrued as something else.

One of the first things I did, when I became the indisputable owner of the coat, was to unpick the seams and sew them up again. I had already made up my mind to establish in no uncertain terms right from the outset who was master, and this seemed as good a way as any of doing so. I have certainly had no trouble of a disciplinary nature in any way since, nor any sign of it. On the contrary the coat has served me well and faithfully over many years and I see no grounds for supposing that such will not be equally the case for many more. I certainly – for those who may be casting covetous eyes towards it – have no intention whatever of parting with the coat. (Except, of course, after I have passed over – and then only by proxy).

Prediction

Compilation One: Anatomy of Bewilderment, 2009.
Previously unpublished.

What do you expect to be doing on eighteenth of February next?

Well…

Round the corner for a pound of best butter, perhaps.

Something of that order…yes…it's quite a possibility.

And then down to the coast for a quick dip in the briny before giving a lick of paint to the side of the garage no doubt.

Yes, I wouldn't be at all surprised if that were not the scenario on the day in question.

The Private Lives of Some Very Great Thinkers Indeed

Snippets Two, BBC Radio 3, 15 March 1983. Revised 2006.

Swedenborg, we are told, saw God as infinite love and infinite wisdom and the end of creation as the approximation of man to God. But though this was undoubtedly one side of Swedenborg, it was not the only side. There was another side: the side that liked to put up shelves and to see to the ceiling where the plaster was coming away. Religion and philosophy were every bit as important in their own way, but, basically, they were there for Swedenborg as something to turn to in the small hours when it wasn't on to go banging about with a hammer, as there were people living upstairs. So often a theologian is, in essence, a kind of handyman manqué who, but for the neighbours, would have been building a cocktail cabinet with bevelled edges and a veneer finish, but has turned to the study of the eternal verities out of frustration: frustration at being unable to get the wood; frustration because he would no sooner get going than there'd be the usual thumping on the wall leaving him with no option but to down tools and start thinking about God again. One is reminded here of Schopenhauer, who, living as he did in a terraced house, had neighbours on either side. It made a quite spectacular difference to his heating bills. He was paying less than half, and this was why he stayed. But the opportunities for making things were seriously curtailed, and it is small wonder that he should have put forward the view that God, freewill and the immortality of the soul are illusions. Rousseau, who spent the better part of his life working up in the attic on that full-scale model of a Spanish galleon, solved the problem of noise by doing it, as we know, in raffia-work. It is possible there were complaints even so. But if there were, no record of them has come down to us. It is worth remarking here, perhaps, that Rousseau's reputation for being hopeless, galleon apart, at anything requiring manual dexterity was largely undeserved. True, he fell off a roof while trying to put some tiles back on, and in doing so, brought another sixteen down with him, and half the guttering. But it was a more or less isolated incident and the kind of thing that could happen to anybody. It has, nevertheless, tended to count against him amongst historians less than sympathetic to Rousseau's pretensions as a handyman. One thing about which there has never been any dispute is that he could lay lino. There are those who would say 'after a fashion', adding that this does not make him the greatest handyman of all time, even if true. But he could do more than lay lino. He could unblock a drain. No outstanding achievement perhaps, except that he had a way of doing it with a broomhandle that impressed those looking on and excited a certain amount of, sometimes grudging, admiration. The real yardstick, surely, is whether you would have had Rousseau in if anything needed doing. Not, if one is being perfectly honest, as a first choice, admittedly, but I would, for my part, have Rousseau every time if it were a choice between him and Freud. Freud's behaviour on a roof is something about which the less said the better. It was, as apologists for Freud are never tired of pointing out, in the middle of the night. And he was taken short. But you don't, in those circumstances, clamber up through the skylight and make water in the first receptacle you see. One is at liberty to accept his explanation that he thought it had been put there for the purpose, but I'm convinced he knew perfectly well what it was put there for. It was put there to measure rainfall and it is almost superfluous to point out that, once the rainfall figures have been distorted, it can affect the whole climactic picture virtually in perpetuity. To go off next morning without a word to anyone, knowing this, is, to my mind, inexcusable. It invalidates his entire corpus.

Renoir

Compilation One: Anatomy of Bewilderment, 2009.
Previously unpublished.

We all recall, do we not, that story of some boorish journalist asking Renoir how with such arthritic hands he was able to hold a brush. Renoir is reputed to have replied 'I paint with my prick.'

How widespread was this practice? And, perhaps more to the point, what was the likely state of the member whilst in use for this purpose? Ernst Grünberg, in his long-awaited *Renoir and Other Masters: A Study in Technique*, has this to say:

> It is at first sight doubtful whether any masterpiece worthy of the name could ever have been produced in its entirety with the brush fastened to a limp member. Any attempt to swing the thing about at random with the brush tied to the end of it, hitting the canvas where it touched and splashing paint here, there and everywhere, could not but be death to any kind of worthwhile artistic endeavour, and is perhaps the most cogent of the arguments against adopting this technique in the first place, though a succession of well-judged hip movements, perfected perhaps over a period of time by practice with some kind of hula-hoop, and executed with a degree of panache and vigour, might, in an artist of genius, produce good work notwithstanding.

An interesting theory that has recently been advanced in this connection is that Michaelangelo might well have adopted this very technique whilst working on the ceiling of the Sistine Chapel. There is a story, which may well be apocryphal, that shortly before embarking on this major work, he had been watching a friend whitewash a ceiling in this way whilst lying on his back on some scaffolding. On any other hypothesis than that the member was erect, it is hard to envisage how this could have been done, since the thing would otherwise have required both splints and a system of stay-wires somewhat in the manner of a present-day television mast. But this poses difficulties. Splints and staywires would severely have restricted the freedom of movement necessary to a fully achieved work. Renoir, moreover, would have been sitting or standing at the easel and, unless one is to assume the presence of a young assistant, trained in Renoir's methods, whose duty it was to move the canvas about at the end of the stationary brush, we must presuppose some degree of flexibility to have been available to Renoir. Grünberg goes further:

> Arising from this, it is perhaps not altogether surprising to note, by inference from the nature of so many of his canvases, that Renoir's studio was more or less permanently graced with several members of the fair sex in a state of nature. What more likely, I would suggest, than that these often quite delectable young women were there to perform for Renoir much the same function as was performed some three centuries before by those handsome and personable young men known to have been present on the scaffolding with Michaelangelo, whose sexual proclivities were, of course, of a radically different kind from those of Renoir but who, like Renoir, had, by virtue of the technique he had chosen to employ, to be in a state of constant arousal. We have it on record, attested by photographs taken of Renoir in his later years, that he is frequently to be seen in fine weather sitting at his easel (always with his back to us!) *outside* his studio. Is this, one is tempted to conjecture, because, the years having begun to take their toll, the number of nubile young women needed to achieve the desired effect would have been such that there was no longer room in the studio for the artist himself, who would be compelled to have recourse to such glimpses as could be had, through the window or through a hole bored in the wall, of the scene within? Too little has perhaps been said of the single-minded devotion of these nubile young women (unsung heroines of art, as they have justly been called), hanging seductively from the rafters and striking poses of a quite breathtakingly indecorous kind in their efforts to keep the master in a state of adequate arousal. It is perhaps safe to say that, but for the dedication of such splendid accomplices, many an ageing artist's bolder brush strokes would have been far lower down on the canvas than, in the event, they finally were.

(One is left to speculate on the endowment of such miniaturists as had recourse to the technique.)

MAKE THIS A BUMPER XMAS FOR EVERYONE!!

Christmas is not Christmas without its toll of dead on the roads - are you equipped to play your part?

leisure promotions

- will tamper with your brakes
- will interfere with your steering
- will loosen vital nuts and bolts

BUT ONLY YOU CAN GET SUFFICIENTLY DRUNK AND INCAPABLE TO DRIVE OFF WITHOUT NOTICING.

Send for our special Christmas Handbook :

Hints for Lethal Maniacs

It will tell you what to drink, when to drink, where to drink and how much to drink.

YOU MAY THINK YOU KNOW ALREADY - BUT DO YOU? DON'T LEAVE IT TO CHANCE : MAKE SURE

REMEMBER ●

HUNDREDS OF DEAD AND MAIMED WILL BE DEPENDING ON PEOPLE LIKE YOU THIS FESTIVE SEASON !

DON'T LET THEM DOWN !

(A Dredgekind & Grodmark Advertisement)

The Seabed

Compilation One: Anatomy of Bewilderment, 2009.
Previously unpublished.

A Mr Yarmouth wanting a donation to The Mission to Deep-Sea Fish of which he is honorary chairman. Offers to come here and show me his snorkel. Decline but enter into conversation about his work. Suggest he must be fairly conversant with the seabed.

'I work there. Sea bass, mainly, in my case. We all specialise. Different fish, different approach. They don't all come to salvation along the same path, any more than you or I do. But we all work together in cahoots with one another. All toiling, as you might say, in the same vineyard. The same oyster bed. And of course to the same end.'

Ask how fish react to seeing him in a snorkel.

'They think it's how we look.

'It must give them a somewhat distorted picture of things as they are on dry land.

'Are we not all to some extent limited in our understanding of the universe we live in, Mr Crompton? How many of us know at first hand what goes on inside a volcano at the moment of erupting? Very much a closed book to nine out of ten of us. Geologists, experts…they all discourse learnedly on it…but have they *been* there? Start to probe and the answer as often as not is "Well, not, in so many words, in person, since you ask." And if you pursue the matter, they start shuffling their feet and looking sheepish. Mutter something none too convincingly about having been laid up with a boil on their bottom, but are fully intending to get round to it eventually.'

He tells me he was on the radio a week or two ago, talking about his work. He was inspired apparently by an Isabel Hopkinson whose book *Underwater Missionary* has become something of a classic.

Snippets

BBC Radio 3, 3 April 1982

1

What is it about the dromedary? There was this great-uncle of mine, whose life was devoted to them. Indeed, it was his overmastering passion for the dromedary which more than anything else carried him halfway round the world in search of the ibex. It was a search that took him to almost every corner of the globe except the mountains of southern Europe, which are its natural habitat. As a result, he not only failed to find the ibex, but had no time for more than a passing glance at the dromedary either. He was very conscious of a sense of failure, and one can see why.

2

It has been put to me that we should be sending harmoniums rather than other aid to the developing countries of Africa. Such a move, it is argued, could bring about an upsurge of nostalgia there for the good old peaceful hymn-singing missionary days such as would be like a refreshing and revitalising bush fire in a parched and arid desert. There is, too, the beautiful and moving symbolism inherent in the harmonium's keyboard, where black notes dwell side by side with white in perfect harmony, and out of their very proximity make divine music. What more seductive concept could there be?

3

What has happened to old-fashioned chivalry? There was a time when it was to all intents and purposes *de rigueur* for any man of breeding to take his teeth out before giving his inamorata a lovebite. In these days of conservative dentristy, fewer and fewer people have this option open to them, alas, and this particular form of courtesy has become, like so much else, a thing of the past. One is left to ponder on whether progress is a desirable thing.

4

The only decent pair of shoes I have were bought cheap at a sale, and are all right until the wet weather starts. I suppose I should count myself lucky not to have been fobbed off with them a couple of hundred million years ago. Sloshing about in the primeval swamp in them without galoshes, they'd have been ruined first time out. There may well, it is true, have been duckboards, but it's unlikely there'd have been enough, and such as there were would for the most part have been earmarked for use by the brontosauri. No, it would have been murder, there's no two ways about it.

5

Dick Whittington! Finest man whose name ever began with a 'W'! Three times Lord Mayor of London within minutes of arriving there as a penniless orphan with nothing but an Alsatian dog for company. Or cat, was it? Either way, no more splendid figure has ever hit the universe fair and square in the solar plexus since Halley's Comet lit off for Blackpool the day its mother died. (And was never seen alive again.) (Except the once, through a telephoto lens, eating a banana.) It gives one fresh hope somehow.

6

I have been looking at the famous painting by Giotto of St Francis preaching to the birds outside Assisi, and trying, not for the first time, to identify the large bird in the middle. *Is* it a red-necked phalarope? Opinions vary. Friends I have canvassed think it may be a Bronze-Breasted Turkey. At all events, there are no penguins to be seen. Hardly surprising, since it would seem scarcely worth a penguin's while to come traipsing all the way to Assisi from the Arctic Circle just to listen to what might well turn out on arrival to be a rather indifferent sermon, briskly though admittedly they walk. I think they must all be local birds.

7

Sixteen. That was the age at which Lady Jane Grey was beheaded in 1554. One wonders how many youngsters of that age would be willing to come forward today in similar circumstances. Precious few. In fact, the average teenager of my acquaintance these days, if you were to go up to him and ask him to put his head on the block with a view to having it cut off, would look at you as if you'd taken leave of your senses. The post-war Labour Government, with its free milk and orange juice, has a lot to answer for.

8

I am wondering if I should take up Morris dancing. I am not particularly keen, but if it would help me to fulfil myself…realise my potential… I would certainly give it a whirl, as they say. On the other hand, the last thing I want is to start to realise my potential only to find I have none. I prefer to imagine it lying there dormant. Hibernating. Waiting for the better weather. If Morris dancing is going to rob me of my illusions, I don't think I want to know. It could do more harm than good. Perhaps I should go back to the drawing board on this one.

9

'A man of considerable stature in his own right as a piano-tuner, he also stuffed owls.' I have been on the *qui vive* for owls for as long as I can remember with some such epitaph for myself as this in mind, but they seem somehow to elude me, perhaps sensing a certain disturbing *je ne sais quoi* in my manner, and feeling less than sanguine as to my motives. Useless to assure them that I have their best long-term interests at heart, and accordingly I am starting to get seriously to grips with the piano *faute de mieux.*

10

A psychologist friend has been explaining to me the rationale behind those Aldwych farces of yesteryear in which someone's trousers would at some point invariably fall down. It seems that, so far from being meant as a joke, these farces were serious psychological studies of a surprisingly neglected phenomenon, which afflicts men of a certain age whose braces, having somehow become twisted at birth, and so subjected to prolonged strain, have grown so weakened over the years that they are constantly on the point of giving way, with humiliating results. At my age, I find this slightly disturbing.

11

How did there come to be an egg stain on the epaulette, of all things, of the naval dress uniform I hired the other day in order to impersonate an Admiral of the Fleet for gain? It would take an acrobatically messy eater to get an egg stain there, you'd think. Someone coming up to him from behind as he was in the act of bringing the spoon with egg in it to his mouth, and so causing him to turn his head, bringing the spoon round with him, as it were. And then, in his surprise, tilting the spoon and spilling egg on his shoulder. It's anybody's guess.

12

It is quite true that we are all abject sinners in the sight of God, and it is both right and proper that we should come to Him in a spirit of humility, with the recognition of that truth in our hearts. But, this having been said, it's an altogether different matter to go swaggering into the confessional, like Jim Phelps, shouting 'Pin your ears back, father, and get a load of this!' The spirit of competitiveness, however acceptable elsewhere, is, as I see it, altogether out of place when one is seeking God's forgiveness, and any priest at all worth his salt will point this out in no uncertain terms to any penitent trying it on in this way.

13

Am I alone in believing myself to have been switched in my cradle? If so, I could well be Muhammed Ali. (And he could be me. A sobering thought for both of us.) Being switched in one's cradle is, it seems, a far commoner phenomenon than many people realise. A great deal depends on how often it gets done, and at what time of life. If it happens in relative maturity, when one's sense of identity is reasonably well established, the shock to the nervous system can be considerable, but in early childhood, if practised in moderation, it can have quite markedly beneficial results, I am told.

Trips

Ambit #202, October 2010

So I asked him what he had in mind for his future and he said he was very good at tripping people up.

Literally?

Oh, yes. Sending them sprawling.

And that's what he's set his sights on.

Believe it or not.

They get some funny ideas. Youngsters nowadays. You'd no more have dreamt of making a career out of tripping people up in our day than you would of filling hot water bottles with hard-boiled eggs.

It's a whole different mindset.

There we go.

In our day it was dropping candlegrease onto hot cross buns.

My particular passion as I remember was arranging water beetles in order of size. That would have been the road I'd have gone down if things had panned out differently. But my father died unexpectedly and I had no choice but to take over the business. We were one of the leading firms specialising in multiplying ninety-three by forty-two. Gave me the opportunity to introduce one or two overdue changes. Adding the square root of a hundred and eighty-nine was one of them.

More than a touch of the maverick about me in those days!

Anyway, I said to him 'I'm not going to be the one to stand in your way if it's what you've set your heart on.'

Sees the thing catching on. Makes a packet, retires early and uses his newfound wealth to give donkey rides to Javanese orphans in Ethiopia. That was the scenario.

All very fine and public spirited, I suppose. Realistically, though…in this day and age…with inflation going through the roof and bankruptcies at a record high…how many people are going to rush to pay out good money in order to be tripped up and made to fall flat on their face?

Well…

However deftly it's done.

Refreshing change frankly to see signs of genuine commitment amongst the young these days. Whatever form it takes. And unlikelier things after all have been known to catch on. In quite a big way sometimes.

Will he have the maturity and strength of character to carry it off? That's the crux.

Well…time will tell.

AN IMAGINATIVE NEW VENTURE

BY

leisure promotions

Experience-of-the-Month Club

leisure promotions Experience-of-the-Month Club has been newly formed with the object of allowing members the opportunity to enjoy the unparalleled services already offered by **leisure promotions** on specially favourable terms.

Membership NOW entitles you to take part in this month's Experience-of-the-Month FREE (Fee to non-members : 10 guineas)

The first **leisure promotions** activity to be made available to members is

A VISIT TO A PRISONER in a CONDEMNED CELL

JOIN NOW TO TAKE ADVANTAGE OF SPECIAL PRIVILEGES

Private Eye #26, 14 December 1962

Twins

Ambit #202, October 2010

You and your brother are identical twins, I gather.

That's right.

How identical in fact are you?

Totally. It's impossible to tell us apart.

You resemble one another in other words.

Yes.

On a regular basis…?

Oh, yes.

Which of you on the whole does most of the resembling?

We take it in turns.

One day he'll resemble you, and the next day…

… I resemble him.

So in other words the resembling's going on all the time.

Absolutely.

Fascinating.

PLANS TO ABOLISH THE DEATH PENALTY
ARE AT PRESENT UNDER CONSIDERATION.
IF THESE ARE CARRIED THROUGH

YOU MAY NEVER HAVE another CHANCE

TO EAVESDROP ON   a condemned man's last conversation with a close relative

BE PRESENT   when he learns there can be no further hope of a reprieve!

WATCH OUT   for every tiny flicker of emotion as it passes across his face at a moment of greater than usual stress

OBSERVE   at close quarters HIS reaction to YOUR presence!!

plus

A UNIQUE OPPORTUNITY TO

LISTEN IN   as he dictates a full confession for publication in the Press

HEAR IT   from him at first-hand, unedited and unabridged, EXACTLY AS HE SPEAKS IT, down to the smallest tremor in his voice

SEE IT   actually being taken down in front of of you by an ace crime reporter from London's famous Fleet Street for publication in a well-known Sunday newspaper

THESE WILL BE SOME OF THE HIGHLIGHTS OF
AN EXPERIENCE YOU WILL NEVER FORGET!!
DON'T WAIT TILL SUNDAY TO READ ABOUT IT
BE THERE IN THE FLESH NOW ! !
(A Dredgekind and Grodmark Advertisement)

Unfounded Optimism!

Compilation One: Anatomy of Bewilderment, 2009.
Previously unpublished.

First grand pianos, then, hard on the heels of that, dead poets –
the one, as ever, leading all too predictably to the other. That old
magpie instinct once more rearing its unsavoury head. In pursuit
of this new craving, you entered Westminster Abbey, crowbar
in hand, intent upon prising Wordsworth, or some other poet of
comparable stature, loose from his resting-place in Poets' Corner.

Your avowed aim, we are invited to believe, was to make use of
him as a door-stop. Nor can it be denied that there is a certain *je
ne sais quoi* about keeping a door open with an erstwhile poetic
genius. A certain cachet attaches to it. You may well say…indeed
have said…that this was not your object at all. That you were
looking simply and solely for something to prop up against a
wall. A not uncommon aspiration, perhaps. I dare say we should
all like to have a dead poet leaning against the wall, or propped
up against the mantelpiece. Chance, some might say, would be
a fine thing.

It was unfortunate that the verger by whom you were intercepted
whilst attempting to realise these aspirations was open to bribery.
Money having changed hands, you were given *carte blanche*
to help yourself to such poets as took your fancy. And, in the
absence of any sense of proportion whatsoever, help yourself you
accordingly did – to not one, but to some sixteen or seventeen
distinguished men of letters, each of whom finished up inside a
cardboard box. It has in all probability never crossed your mind
to ask yourself what sort of a world we would be living in if this
way of behaving were to become general.

Nor is the situation improved by your having seen fit to house
– albeit as an interim measure – each of these seventeen or
eighteen distinguished men of letters in a cardboard box with
the word 'Winalot' engraved on its side. One would be hard
put to imagine any action more calculated to do severe and
lasting damage to our whole poetic heritage. It requires but little
imagination to envisage the likely outcome when the ordinary
man in the street, not particularly conversant perhaps with the

poetic tradition that has been handed down to him, opens up a cardboard box in full expectation of finding a reasonably varied and representative assortment of dog biscuits inside, and comes, not upon the dog biscuits he had been so confidently anticipating, but upon Swinburne instead. And what of his dog? There is no nutritive value of any account in a long-dead poet compared with what would be found in biscuits produced for the purpose by a reputable manufacturer with an eye to the health of the dog for whom a properly balanced diet is of prime importance. The spectacle of some uncombed Irish wolfhound or Scottish terrier turning away in disdain or indifference from a poet of the stature of Browning or Dryden can do nothing but harm to the cause of poetry, and a nation's poetic heritage can suffer irreparable damage in consequence.

You will say, indeed counsel has already said on your behalf, that the cardboard box with which we are concerned here contained not Swinburne, but Wordsworth. The ordinary man, not versed in the ways of poetry, will in all probability be unable to tell the difference between Wordsworth and Swinburne, or between either of them and Tennyson. But – and this is where the insidiousness lies for all to see – he can very easily tell the difference between any one of them and a dog biscuit!

Nor is this an end of the matter. A poet who has been dead for some hundred years or more can reasonably expect to be by now in full rigor mortis. Indeed, the thought must have crossed your mind that such a poet could well be leaned against the wall without any danger of subsiding into an ungainly heap the moment you let go of him, and it was doubtless this which in part prompted your choice in the matter. It leads us, however, to ask how these same poets were rendered pliable enough to be folded up in such a way as to be got inside a cardboard box. 'I boiled them,' was your reply when the question was put to you. And that, we are invited to believe, did the trick. If I, or someone else, in other words, were wanting, for some private reason of our own, to render a long-dead poet pliable enough to go into a cardboard box, we would first have to furnish ourselves with a receptacle large enough, and with some form of heating apparatus capable of providing sufficient water at the requisite temperature, and then arrive at a means of poking these poets down whenever they rose, as rise they frequently must, to the surface. In your case, we are given to understand, you made use for this purpose of, in your own words, 'a bit of old broomhandle'. I cannot forbear to remark that it would have saved you, and this court, a great deal of time and trouble had you taken the broomhandle you were at such pains to furnish yourself with, and leaned that against the wall instead.

A Visit to Ken Wood

Compilation One: Anatomy of Bewilderment, 2009.
Previously unpublished.

And who is this fellow?

Rembrandt, Otto.

Ah.

It's the famous self-portrait.

Rembrandt was a painter…?

Oh, yes. Arguably one of the greatest masters ever to have put paint to canvas.

Not Leonardo da Vinci?

Leonardo da Vinci too.

Ah. So who, then, was Rimsky-Korsakov?

Rimsky-Korsakov was a composer, Otto.

A *composer*, you say?

That's right.

But I was under the impression that that was Haydn.

Haydn, too, Otto. They were both composers.

So how does one tell them apart?

I think Rimsky-Korsakov was the one…wasn't he?…with glasses.

That was Mendelssohn.

Yes, I know Mendelssohn wore glasses, but…

So did Schubert.

Schubert, did I hear you say?

Thickset man. Darkish. Rather tousled hair. My height.

But forgive me… I'm becoming a little confused here…how does Rembrandt fit into all this?

He fits in in the sense that…well…

He would appear to have been a somewhat unmusical man. Would I be on the right track there?

There's a story that he had a tin whistle. Though whether he found time to make full use of it.

Oh, the artistic world! I despair! Shall I ever get to understand it?

MAKE THIS A BUMPER
NEW YEAR
BLACKMAIL
A FRIEND FOR
CHARITY

A Dredgekind & Grodmark Ad.

War

Compilation One: Anatomy of Bewilderment, 2009.
Previously unpublished.

I've had this idea. It came to me in the night. About war.

Is it practical?

I think it's practical.

All right. Let's chew it over then.

What I was thinking…in the event of a nuclear war…people's teeth could get blown out, couldn't they?

In one or two cases, yes, I dare say, they could.

So if they're going to get blown out anyway…

Go on.

…why not take them out beforehand?

For safe keeping.

Well, partly, yes.

I don't think I'm altogether following you.

Well…once you've taken their teeth out…

Yes?

…you can say…

Ah… I think I can see which way your mind is working… 'Either you shake hands and make up here and now… or that's the last you see of your teeth.'

If it makes people think twice about going to war.

I'm not altogether happy about the ethics of it. It smacks a little bit of blackmail.

Yes, I suppose it does.

Putting that to one side for the moment…there's a practical aspect to it as well. Here we are after all with a couple of nations who for some reason have got their dander up to the extent that they're ready to go for one another with state-of-the-art weapons. Is it altogether realistic in that situation to think either side is going to be in the mood to sit down in a dentist's chair while someone they may never have seen before starts taking all their teeth out?

If it's for their own good.

Well…

And the good of humanity.

Perhaps.

You'd have to re-educate people, obviously.

Those who were willing to be re-educated.

The ones who wouldn't listen would simply have to be got into the chair by brute force. It smacks of high-handedness, I know, but if they haven't got the sense. And it would pay off in the long run. People would be a lot less trigger-happy.

Bearing in mind that something like this would require major legislation. It'd cause a major outcry if one took it on oneself to confiscate a nation's teeth without proper authority. It would be seen as an affront to individual freedom.

War itself is an affront to individual freedom.

Yes. You've obviously put some thought into this.

Why I Write

Contemporary Dramatists (St James Press, 1973)

The question that, as a writer, one is asked more frequently than any other is the question as to why of all things it should be plays that one has chosen to bring forth rather than, say, novels or books about flying saucers. The answer in my own case lies, I think, in the fact that there is one incomparable advantage which the play, as a form, has over the novel and the book about flying saucers; and this is that there are not anything like as many words in it. For a writer condemned from birth to draw upon a reservoir of energy such as would barely suffice to get a tadpole from one side of a tea-cup to the other, such a consideration cannot but be decisive. Poetry admittedly has in general fewer words still, and for this reason is on the face of it an even more attractive discipline; but alas I have even less gift for that than I have for writing plays, and if I had the gift for it, it would be only a matter of weeks before I came up against the ineluctable truth that there is just not the money in it that there is in plays. Not that, the way I write them, there is all that much money in those either.

As for methods of work, what I do is to husband with jealous parsimony such faint tremors of psychic energy as can sometimes be coaxed out of the permanently undercharged batteries I was issued with at birth, and when I have what might be deemed a measurable amount, to send it coursing down the one tiny channel where with any luck it might do some good. Here it deposits its wee pile of silt, which I allow to accumulate, with the barely perceptible deliberation of a coral reef to the point where it may one day recognise itself with a start of surprise as the small and unpretentious magnum opus it had all along been tremulously aspiring to.

As for why one does it there are various reasons – all of them fairly absurd. There is one's ludicrously all-embracing sense of guilt mainly. I walk the streets in perpetual fear and trepidation, like someone who expects, round the very next corner, to meet his just deserts at the hands of a lynch mob carried away by fully justified indignation. To feel *personally* responsible not only for every crime, ever atrocity, every act of inhumanity that has ever been perpetrated since the world began, but for those as well that have not as yet been so much as contemplated, is something which only Jesus Christ and I can ever have experienced to anything like the same degree. And it goes a long way to account for what I write and why I write it. For not only must one do what one can by writing plays to make amends for the perfidy of getting born; one must also, in the interests of sheer self-preservation, keep permanently incapacitated by laughter as many as possible of those who would otherwise be the bearers of a just and terrible retribution. One snatches one's reprieve quite literally laugh by laugh.

My plays are about life – life as I see it. Which is to say that they are all in their various ways about a man trying to get a partially inflated rubber lilo into a suitcase slightly too small to take it even when *un*inflated. Like most Englishmen, of which I am proud to be one, I have a love of order tempered by a deep and abiding respect for anarchy, and what I would one day like to bring about is that perfect balance between the two which I believe to be peculiarly in the nature of English genius to arrive at. I doubt very much whether I ever shall, but it is nevertheless what I would like to do.

N.F. SIMPSON

Window

Sketches for Radio, BBC Radio 3, 23 July 1974

ARNOLD
....

MOTHER
....

FATHER
....

Well furnished top floor room.

ARNOLD, a put-upon young man, is staring out of the window through glasses with thick pebble lenses.

MOTHER is writing a letter at a small elegant writing table. FATHER is sitting in a big, comfortable leather armchair, reading The Times.

MOTHER: What are you doing, Arnold?

ARNOLD: I'm looking out of the window, mother.

MOTHER: Trying to see across the road, I suppose.

ARNOLD: Yes, mother.

> *Pause.*

MOTHER: Other people looking out of a window like that would be able to see virtually to the other side of London.

ARNOLD: Other people are not shortsighted, mother, are they?

MOTHER: *(Half to herself.)* The thickest lenses in his glasses that anyone has ever seen since the world began, and all he can do is see to the other side of the road through them.

ARNOLD: If you're shortsighted, mother, you're shortsighted.

MOTHER: Other people are shortsighted, Arnold. I'm shortsighted. So is your father. But we don't all of us give in to it.

FATHER: Willpower. That's all it needs. The ability to make up your mind to do a thing, and then do it.

MOTHER: Instead of just standing there in the hope that if you wait long enough the view will come to you of its own accord. It won't. You've got to go out after it.

ARNOLD: I'm going out after it as best I can, mother.

Pause.

MOTHER: The same with your club foot. And your partial deafness. And your tendency to knock into furniture all the time.

ARNOLD: The only reason I knock into furniture is that I can't see where I'm going. If I could see where I was going, I wouldn't knock into it.

MOTHER: It does no good either to you or to the furniture.

Pause.

ARNOLD: If you don't want me tripping over the furniture, why don't you put it somewhere other than just inside the door every time? If you put it somewhere out of the way, I might be able to walk into a room without barking my shin every time.

Pause.

MOTHER: There's such a thing as trying to overcome a handicap, instead of giving in to it every time.

FATHER: Being weak and spineless.

MOTHER: And wanting everything made easy all the time.

Pause.

FATHER: You want to make the effort to exert yourself a little bit.

Pause.

MOTHER: A small fortune we must have spent on opticians, one way and another, and what is there to show for it?

ARNOLD: At least I can see the window! Even if I can't see through it.

Pause.

MOTHER: We haven't begrudged what we've spent, either. But it would be nice to have some kind of success to show for it.

ARNOLD: I'm not responsible, am I, mother, for being shortsighted! I'm not shortsighted for fun!

MOTHER: One only wishes one could be sure.

FATHER: If you're not responsible for it, who, in heaven's name, is?

MOTHER: Somebody else, presumably.

Pause.

MOTHER: You realise, don't you, what the end product is going to be, if you go on the way you're doing now?

FATHER: Blind.

MOTHER: Exactly.

FATHER: You start off giving in to shortsightedness, and before you know where you are you're on the slippery slope that leads to total blindness.

MOTHER: Selling matches in the gutter, with twenty-nine or thirty children to support.

FATHER: With his club foot and his deaf aid to keep him company.

MOTHER: Arnold. What are you doing?

ARNOLD flings his glasses to the floor and grinds them underfoot.

MOTHER: You realise don't you, Arnold, that that's your extremely expensive surgical boot you're using to smash your glasses with…

ARNOLD strides unevenly across the room.

ARNOLD: *(Shrill vehemence.)* Sod the pair of you! You can both bugger off out of it, and good riddance to you!

ARNOLD exits, slamming door. There is a loud, reverberating crash outside it.

Pause.

MOTHER moves across to FATHER.

MOTHER: Where did we go wrong, James?

Fade.

With His Bare Hands (formerly The Amazing Deeds of Archbishop Lanfranc)

Snippets Two, BBC Radio 3, 14 March 1983. Revised 2006.

It is well enough known, I dare say, that the present cathedral at Canterbury replaced an earlier building which had been burnt down in 1067, but I, for one, had, until quite recently, always assumed the existing edifice to have been the work of a whole vast army of stonemasons and others labouring together as a doubtless highly organised team. It may be imagined, therefore, with what utterly dumbfounded amazement I learned from the guidebook to the cathedral that it was built in 1070 by Archbishop Lanfranc. One looks up at the enormous edifice in the light of this quite staggering piece of information in absolute stupefaction. What manner of man, one finds oneself asking, can this, in all conscience, have been? It is an achievement, moreover, which, astounding enough in itself, becomes all the more remarkable when one reflects that, unless one is to suppose some kind of indefinitely extended sabbatical, this monumental task would presumably have had to be undertaken by the Archbishop in addition to his routine sacerdotal duties and, accordingly, therefore, one imagines, in the evenings or during those rare weekends when, for one reason or another, his services were not required at the altar. We have to remind ourselves, too, that this was at a time long before the Leaning Tower of Pisa had conferred the accolade of respectability on large-scale deviations from the vertical. In 1070 it was more or less universally accepted that, in order to mean anything at all to succeeding generations, a building had, above all, to be upright, or as near upright as makes no difference. It must be a matter for conjecture whether Lanfranc was fortunate enough to know someone from whom to borrow a spirit-level, but, if, as seems probable, he had to make do with a little brass weight on the end of a piece of string, the success of the enterprise is striking. Nor could his decision to embark on so mammoth an undertaking have been less than a bombshell for

those to whom he confided it. There must have been those who
saw it as evidence that their Archbishop had taken leave of his
senses, and one can readily imagine the efforts that were made,
tactfully, to talk him out of it. But Lanfranc went ahead, and it
must have been with mounting misgiving that those who counted
themselves his friends stood watching the progress of the work
as the diminutive figure high above the ground and in cope and
mitre the more effectively to bear witness to his faith and calling,
heaved and tugged at some more than usually large and awkward
slab of masonry in an attempt to manoeuvre it into position,
possibly by the light of a torch, in inclement weather on some late
autumn evening. Time and again their hearts must have been in
their mouths as they saw him come within an ace, as it must have
seemed, of rupturing himself, with all that would have meant to
the church at a critical moment in her history, and with utter
bafflement they must have turned away as, with uncharacteristic
brusqueness, he time and again refused point blank any offer of
help. At this distance of time one can do no more than hazard a
guess as to what was in his mind. For this was no idle whim on
Lanfranc's part, and with hindsight it is possible to discover what
lay behind so quixotic an undertaking. Lanfranc was Archbishop
of Canterbury at a time when we know the church to have been
riven by strife and dissension, and for an Archbishop intent
on improving his physique the better to hold his own against
ambitious rivals for the primacy what more effective way could
there be than by building a full-sized cathedral to the greater
glory of God? It comes, at all events, as no surprise to learn that
Lanfranc was, from this time onward, increasingly a force to be
reckoned with in the counsels of both church and state, where it
would have been a rash adversary indeed who would venture to
stand out for long against someone with biceps as formidable as
Lanfranc's must by this time have become, and it is fair to assume
that once he had rolled up his sleeves, ostensibly the better to get
to grips with the matter in hand, the motion would have been
carried *nemine contradicente.* If this is true, what a lesson it holds
for those of us who have the welfare of our country at heart today.
It would need no more than a handful of dedicated men and
women imbued with the spirit that was Lanfranc's nine centuries
ago and, provided enough people could be persuaded to come
forward with land and materials, we could have, within a decade,

not only some six or seven additional cathedrals, but, what to my mind is infinitely more important, a small but effective group of well-developed people of both sexes, superbly fit and with the kind of physique that, like Lanfranc's, could be relied upon to carry weight and command respect wherever they might appear. The conspicuous, though not obtrusive, presence at international gatherings of such a body, representing this country and being known to represent this country, could go far towards ensuring that Britain's voice was at long last not only heard but heeded once again in the council chambers of the world.

N.F. SIMPSON

I suppose you've heard…

Oh, no! Don't tell me!

Afraid so.

Did think the last time would be a lesson to him.

So much promise.

What a waste! What a waste!

Compilation One: Anatomy of Bewilderment, 2009. Previously unpublished.

World in Ferment: N.F. Simpson comments on television and current affairs

The Listener, 24 July 1969

Cripplingly expensive though it is to maintain, and subject as it is to all manner of disabilities and malfunctions, the human being – adaptable, self-perpetuating, independent, fully automated, and ingeniously designed to meet the manifold needs of a highly complex society – must unquestionably be the best all-round tool for the job that could ever have been devised. And I am thinking not only of such comparatively simple tasks as populating towns and keeping vehicles constantly on the move between them, vital though this is, but of its capacity for meeting the needs of shops, offices, airfields, power stations, research laboratories, amusement arcades, secret military installations, churches, sports arenas, and an infinity of other greedy claimants for its services. Tough and resilient, it is in constant demand wherever there are peerages to be conferred, rare books to be auctioned, cruel sports to be protested against, cardboard cartons to be disposed of, cattle to be examined for footrot, life insurance to be set against income for tax purposes, paper hats to be worn, wars to be fought, mattresses to be turned, banners to be borne aloft, big game to be hunted, sardines to be put into tins, Papal nuncios to be received, or lavatories to be sprinkled with Harpic. In fact, it is the staggering diversity of the uses to which it can be put that holds out the brightest hope for the future. Nothing so versatile and useful can possibly become obsolete while there are so many tails needing so many eager, willing dogs to wag.

And what tail wags more dogs more effectively than the news and commentary industry, unless it be the social survey industry, with its smokescreen of facts and figures, which must never be allowed to thin out for fear we might catch some hazy glimpse of reality on the other side. With every day that passes, so much more newsprint coming off the rollers, so much more television time stretching into infinity, so many more issues of weekly magazines to be filled at all costs with solemn and boring drivel like this – what is there for the responsible and conscientious world citizen with a proper sense of his duty to civilisation, except to be constantly searching his soul in answer to questions like: Am I leading a truly newsworthy life? How much more newsworthy, with a little effort, could I make it? Am I taking more out of the news media than I am putting in? Am I pulling my weight as a data-generating unit, or is there somewhere a census form in the making which in the fullness of time will find me wanting, a computer yet unborn that may one day go hungry because I fell down on the job? Do I hold enough opinions, or is it possible that I could one day be caught out with a microphone thrust into my face and not a viewpoint to utter? The shame of it. One would hardly feel fit to live.

Not that by living life more newsworthily one could hope to provide more than the raw material. For news is processed fact. It must be urgent, significant, or moving. Fortunately almost anything, by a little judicious messing about or a nicely calculated tone of voice, can be made to seem any or all of these things, so the chronic shortage of things which really are so is not as crippling as it might be. The trouble is that the fantasy world engendered in this way by the news media is inextricably confused for most of us with the real one, and it is one of the commoner fallacies of the present day that newspapers and television broaden our knowledge of the world, whereas the truth is in many ways almost the exact opposite. What we do get is an illusion of being in the know, which, since it operates at something like twenty-fifth hand, is probably standing between most of us and life far more effectively than total ignorance ever did. And with the illusion of being in the know – by virtue of which what was happening down the road is something we never properly got acquainted with because we were finding out about the elections in Madagascar on *Panorama* at the time – go the other illusions of involvement and concern. I am not able to say, for instance, how the total number of homeless people compares now with what it was when *Cathy Come Home* went out, but the deep concern engendered from armchair to armchair in well-appointed house after well-appointed house from one end of the British Isles to the other, when that television programme appeared, was a moving and impressive thing. Could there have been a single publication anywhere for months afterwards which did not carry some expression of outraged indignation, some fierce, well-merited denunciation of some authority or other, some clarion call to action on the part of almost anybody but the writer, whose time was already fully taken up with watching television programmes like *Cathy Come Home* and seeing that his rates stayed down?

It is certainly, I suppose, a way of having one's cake and eating it, but while the illusion flatters our ego by enormously enlarging the scale on which we nowadays imagine ourselves to be operating, it does so at the expense of pointing up our inadequacies at the same time. If the problems of simply keeping one's head above water from day to day are a full-time job for most of us, what in God's name do we flatter ourselves we can do about the ludicrous complexities of the big global issues that we tear ourselves to pieces in helpless frustration over? As one who by temperament is inclined to take life very much as it comes, sidestepping where possible, I am tempted to say that if everyone else did the same, most of the world's troubles would be over. I do see, though, that the remedy might well in a good many respects be worse than the disease, and am not offering it as a serious contribution on this particular issue. The truth nevertheless seems to be that the impulse that carries society along chooses paths which have little or nothing to do with any direction its individual members may have thought they had in mind. So that any current affairs programme that cons us into thinking events are under control is dealing in delusions.

In the last analysis – as they say in this sort of programme – it is in fact the nature of the exercise that is absurd, and not the way the exercise is carried out. It is absurd, and comic, in the way that everything else is absurd and comic. People think that a sense of humour is to do with being able to recognise at a glance what is funny and what is not. It is nothing of the kind. It is a recognition that everything is funny if you look at it in one way rather than another. And one of the ways of making things seem funny to other people is, for some reason, to do an almost, but not quite, exact imitation of them. And this is a matter of noticing mannerisms, and reproducing them with a slight element of caricature. Verbal

N. F. SIMPSON

mannerisms as well as behavioural ones. People call these clichés, and go on about them as if it were some mark of near-illiteracy to make use of them. So what is life supposed to be – an unremitting process of spontaneous creation? Everybody resorts to clichés: how else would speech, or life itself, be possible? But this is not to say that, like everything else that 'grave, censorious, senatorial, soul-possessing Man, erect on his two spindles', manages to bring into being, including the kind of windy pointless chat with which my own quota of column inches is at this very moment being filled, it is not totally absurd and utterly nonsensical. (Is there nothing better, in God's name, that you could be doing than reading this? Or that I could be doing than writing it?) And it is part of one's sense of proportion to recognise that everything, however seriously it may deserve to be taken in one context, is inherently absurd in another. It is particularly salutary to do so in those moments when the human race is on its high horse about being some superior form of creation – than which no spectacle could well be more laughable to anyone in a laughing mood.

This was supposed to have been some kind of introduction to some excerpts from the television programme I wrote called *World in Ferment*, which is a sort of current affairs programme gone slightly mad. So how much of what I have been so tediously going on about here is reflected in the programme itself? The answer is: very little. It just happens that I am the kind of writer who is great at starting things, but never knows how the hell to bring them to an end. With this format one doesn't have to. One just goes on to something else. It seemed quite an inspiration.

World of Books: Where Do We Go From Here?

Private Eye #100, 15 October 1965

WORLD OF BOOKS N.F. SIMPSON

Where do we go from here?

THE ABC RAILWAY GUIDE (SKINNER 8s. 6d.)

Boring, tedious, repetitive. This is my verdict on a book which, for all one's high hopes as yet another edition makes its appearance on the bookstalls, turns out on inspection to be nothing more than the mixture almost exactly as before.

In the first of the three parts into which the book falls, we are treated to a series of variations on the hotel theme. Here the same paucity of inventiveness that left one almost numb with disbelief in earlier versions is again in evidence, contributing once more to a dreariness so monumental as to be virtually beyond description. Seldom, one is left to reflect, can contempt for the reader have reached such heights of sublimity as it does here.

Nor do things noticeably improve in the middle section of the book, where the hero - an unnamed traveller in whose wake we chase hither and thither from one end of the British Isles to the other, and even on occasion to the Continent as well - is again engaged on some nightmare journey the purpose of which is never at any point made clear to us.

It is the final sequence, however, that brings the narrative, sous forme d'indicateur ferroviaire, to its inevitable climax. The hapless hero, by now totally unable by some fatal paralysis of the will to decide where it is he wants to go, or at what time he should make the journey, embarks with demented frenzy upon one abortive attempt after another, driving himself and the reader to the very brink of insanity in the process. Harrowing enough, in all conscience - but it would require the exercise of talents of a far higher order than are displayed here to induce this reader to share the experience through nearly four hundred closely-written pages.

This is clearly the private fantasy of a sick mind. It is the kind of thing, however, for which, if sales are any guide to a book's popularity, there would seem to be a very considerable public; and for that reason alone we can no doubt resign ourselves to seeing it appear on our bookstalls with the same depressing regularity in the future as it has been doing, in edition after edition now, for more than a century past.

N.F. SIMPSON

<u>The ABC Railway Guide (Skinner 8s. 6d.)</u>

Boring, tedious, repetitive. This is my verdict on a book which, for all one's high hopes as yet another edition makes its appearance on the bookstalls, turns out on inspection to be nothing more than the mixture almost exactly as before.

In the first of the three parts into which the book falls, we are treated to a series of variations on the hotel theme. Here the same paucity of inventiveness that left one almost numb with disbelief in earlier versions is again in evidence, contributing once more to a dreariness so monumental as to be virtually beyond description. Seldom, one is left to reflect, can contempt for the reader have reached such heights of sublimity as it does here.

Nor do things noticeably improve in the middle section of the book, where the hero – an unnamed traveller in whose wake we chase hither and thither from one end of the British Isles to the other, and even on occasion to the Continent as well – is again engaged on some nightmare journey the purpose of which is never at any point made clear to us.

It is the final sequence, however, that brings the narrative, *sous forme d'indicateur ferroviaire*, to its inevitable climax. The hapless hero, by now totally unable by some fatal paralysis of the will to decide where it is he wants to go, or at what time he should make the journey, embarks with demented frenzy upon one abortive attempt after another, driving himself and the reader to the very brink of insanity in the process. Harrowing enough, in all conscience – but it would require the exercise of talents of a far higher order than are displayed here to induce this reader to share the experience through nearly four hundred closely-written pages.

This is clearly the private fantasy of a sick mind. It is the kind of thing, however, for which, if sales are any guide to a book's popularity, there would seem to be a very considerable public; and for that reason alone we can no doubt resign ourselves to seeing it appear on our bookstalls with the same depressing regularity in the future as it has been doing, in edition after edition now, for more than a century past.

The Wrapped Gift

The Dick Emery Show, BBC One, 22 October 1977

MAN
....

WIFE
....

SENIOR ASSISTANT
....

MR SIMS
....

Scene One: Bedroom

MAN and WIFE asleep in bed. WIFE begins to stir, reaches up and switches on light over bed. Looks at clock on bedside table. It says ten to three. She reaches down to floor and picks up a small, lavishly wrapped parcel. She gently nudges her sleeping husband.

WIFE: Happy birthday.

He comes sleepily to.

MAN: I beg your pardon?

WIFE: I had it wrapped for you.

MAN: I'd just dropped off. *(Puts on glasses.)* 'To George. A little something to be going on with.' Beautifully wrapped.

WIFE: Do you think so?

MAN: It must have cost you the earth to have it wrapped like this.

WIFE: Well, yes…it wasn't cheap.

MAN: Beautiful job. Thank you very much.

He gives her a light kiss on the forehead, and puts the parcel down.

WIFE: I'm glad you like it. I hoped you would.

WIFE reaches up to put out light.

WIFE: You can take it in on the way to work to have it unwrapped.

MAN: Yes, I will.

WIFE: Then you can find out what's in it.

MAN: Yes. I shall look forward to that.

WIFE: Goodnight.

MAN: Goodnight.

Fade down. Fade up.

MAN switches light on his side and gets out of bed.

WIFE: *(Waking up.)* What are you doing?

MAN: It's no good, Freda. I can't sleep till I find out what's inside.

WIFE: But the unwrapping department won't be open at this time, George.

MAN: I'll knock them up. They won't mind. They're always glad to oblige.

He goes.

WIFE: I hope it's not a wasted journey.

Light out.

Scene Two: Harridge's Gift Unwrapping Department

Twenty-four hour service, as the sign proclaims. It is a plush carpeted salon which, unless you knew otherwise, you would think was in some house of haute couture. The clock on the wall declares it to be three o'clock. A MAN wearing pyjamas under a smart undercoat is standing at the counter. The SENIOR ASSISTANT is behind the counter holding a very expensively wrapped gift.

ASSISTANT: *(Reading the tag attached to the gift.)* 'To George. A little something to be going on with.'

MAN: It's from the wife – for my birthday.

ASSISTANT: And very nice too. *(Examines elaborate wrapping.)* Hmmm. Beautifully wrapped.

MAN: Yes, isn't it. I gather she had it specially done in your gift wrapping department.

ASSISTANT: Ah yes. I thought I recognised their touch. And now you'd like it *un*wrapped.

MAN: Well, yes, you see my wife handed it to me in bed just as I was dropping off and I couldn't sleep for wondering what was inside. So I came round here hotfoot to you.

ASSISTANT: You realise that there is an All Night Gift Unwrappery in Piccadilly.

MAN: Yes, I know that – but I'd prefer you to do it – after all, you're the experts, aren't you.

ASSISTANT: We do have a certain reputation, yes. Well, all right sir, in the circumstances, we will be pleased to assist. We'll do it under our emergency scheme.

MAN: *(Relieved.)* Oh thank you very much.

ASSISTANT: *(Takes up pro-forma and pen.)* Would you like it done while you wait or can we contact you when it's ready?

MAN: Well… I could certainly do with getting back to bed. I mean, although I'm curious to find out what's inside, if you're going to do that for me it does seem a bit superfluous for me to be here as well.

ASSISTANT: A very sensible attitude, sir. *(Makes note.)* Would you want appreciation shown at the moment of unwrapping?

MAN: *(Unsure.)* Oh, well…

ASSISTANT: I would recommend it, sir – it can be a very cold-blooded operation otherwise.

MAN: What would that entail…?

ASSISTANT: Oh, you know… 'What a surprise!', 'Fancy remembering', 'It's what I've always wanted' – that sort of thing. Of course, it would be done by experts who would naturally make a much more effective job of it than you could hope to do yourself.

MAN: Oh, well in that case…

ASSISTANT: In due course, we would obviously send your wife a recorded description of the unpacking with a photograph in full colour so that she can have a permanent record of the occasion.

MAN: Oh, she'd like that.

ASSISTANT: You would presumably want it cherished. It's an optional extra, but it's proving very popular.

MAN: Cherished.

ASSISTANT: Assuming when we unwrap the object, that it turns out to be something you would normally expect to have around as an object of, say, beauty or delight…we could arrange to have it lodged in the Appreciation Room, where one of our trained staff would go down and look lovingly at it every hour, on the hour, from dawn to dusk. Or even more frequently if you prefer.

MAN: Yes, I see…well…

ASSISTANT: For anyone whose time is at a premium, it's very much a boon.

MAN: Well, in that case…yes, by all means.

ASSISTANT: *(Makes another note and turns page.)* Which brings us to the old vexed question of disposal.

MAN: Ah.

ASSISTANT: The policy we normally work to here is that in the ordinary course of events the object inside…whatever it may turn out to be when we unwrap it…will sooner or later, in the daily wear and tear of things, get broken or damaged or otherwise rendered useless, and all we need to know, really, is what you would consider a suitable interval before we arrange for that to happen. And whether you want it, when the time comes, to simply disintegrate in the washing-up water, or be dropped on the floor, or just come apart in someone's hands.

MAN: Yes. I see.

ASSISTANT: It's entirely up to you. Or we could have something heavy fall on it from a height.

He points up to where a two-ton weight is ready poised for such purposes.

MAN: Could it be knocked off a shelf with a feather duster at all?

ASSISTANT: Certainly. Nothing easier. *(Makes note.)*

MAN: By a French maid…with frilly…

ASSISTANT: Yes, I suppose that would be possible. *(Makes note.)* I'll talk to our fetish department. I assume that once it is broken you'd like it put straight into the dustbin.

MAN: Oh, yes… I think so. No point in patching it up. Not at that stage.

ASSISTANT: Oh, none at all. Now what sort of timescale would you prefer?

MAN: Timescale?

ASSISTANT: For the irreparable damage to take place. In six months time…a year? *(Shakes parcel gently and holds it to his ear.)* Until it's been through the X-ray machine it's hard to know what its normal life span would be. But if you wanted the whole thing over and done with fairly quickly, we could arrange to have it appreciated more intensively over a shorter period, and we could then get it into the dustbin for you in a matter of weeks or even days.

MAN: My word!

ASSISTANT: Unless of course you wanted to take advantage of our special fifty pound Jubilee Souvenir Service – in which case we could simply throw it straight into the dustbin for you now without even unwrapping it.

MAN: Well, I…

ASSISTANT: Many people think it's money well spent for what amounts to a very real saving in time and trouble.

MAN: *(Coming to decision.)* Yes, I'm sure you're right. *(Takes out cheque book.)* I assume you'll take a cheque?

ASSISTANT: Yes of course, sir. Make it out to Harridge's, please.

MAN starts to write cheque.

ASSISTANT: *(Calls.)* Mr Sims! *(To MAN.)* Mr Sims is very much a specialist in the field of gift disposal. He's been with us for some years and I'm sure you'll be delighted with the way he handles the operation.

The MAN hands over the cheque.

ASSISTANT: Thank you, sir. Ah, here's Mr Sims now.

MR SIMS enters with a shiny new dustbin. He arrives at counter and nods at MAN.

SIMS: Good evening, sir.

He lifts the lid and the SENIOR ASSISTANT lightly tosses the gift into the bin.

MR SIMS replaces the lid and goes off.

ASSISTANT: We're often asked how we can do it for the money, but that's our secret. Anyway… Mr, er…?

MAN: Cartwright.

ASSISTANT: …any other time we can be of service, don't hesitate to come in – even in the daytime!

MAN: Thank you.

He turns to go off as the SENIOR ASSISTANT completes the paperwork and SIMS reappears with gift still wrapped.

SIMS: I wonder if we don't do too much for them sometimes.

ASSISTANT: It's the spirit of service that counts.

Takes gift from SIMS and restores it to shelf of similar gifts of different shapes and sizes, which we now see for the first time.

Your Flame, Or Mine?

Sketches for Radio, BBC Radio 3, 23 July 1974

BASIL
....
URSULA
....

Balcony. Moonlight.

BASIL and URSULA. Strangled upper-class voices.

BASIL: I was…admiring…your matches, Ursula.

URSULA: Oh…those.

BASIL: Swedish, aren't they?

URSULA: Yes.

BASIL: I thought they were Swedish.

> *Pause.*

URSULA: Try one.

BASIL: May I?

URSULA: Of course.

BASIL: I should like to very much.

URSULA: Take one out. Rub it along the side of the box.

> *A match is struck, and the flame spurts up.*

BASIL: It's not hard, is it, to see why people go for them.

URSULA: It's the flame.

BASIL: Yes.

URSULA: The flame that spurts up when you strike it against the box.

> *Pause.*

BASIL: Has it ever struck you, Ursula, how very, very much more fascinating other people's matches always are than the matches one owns oneself?

URSULA: It seems like that to you, too?

BASIL: So often. So very, very often. *(Pause.)* There are days, out at Tottenham, when one gets absolutely sick of one's matches. One couldn't really care whether one strikes them or not.

Pause.

URSULA: Did you…did you say… Tottenham, Basil…?

BASIL: Yes, my dearest.

URSULA: How strange…how strange that I never knew.

BASIL: Never knew, my love?

URSULA: Never knew that you came from…from Tottenham.

BASIL: Perhaps I should have told you.

URSULA: Oh, no. That would have spoiled everything. It's so much more romantic like this.

BASIL: Is it, my sweet?

URSULA: I've always dreamt…does this sound terribly girlish and silly, Basil? …that one day I would meet someone who came from Tottenham.

BASIL: All my life I have come from Tottenham. Ever since… ever since the day I was born.

URSULA: Has it…has it changed much?

BASIL: Oh, terribly, it's frightfully, frightfully different from what it was.

URSULA: How sad.

BASIL: It's changed beyond all recognition since it was first mentioned in the *Domesday Book*. Even the people have changed. They're different too.

URSULA: And Hotspur? Is he still living at Tottenham?

BASIL: Only, alas, when playing at home.

URSULA: May I, Basil…may I…perhaps…come out there…one day…?

BASIL: Oh, Ursula…would you? Would you really come out there?

URSULA: Oh, yes, Basil. I should like to do that. I should like to do that more than anything.

BASIL: And I could…perhaps…show you my…my *Whitaker's Almanack*…

URSULA: Is it…is it the original *Whitaker's Almanack*?

BASIL: It's the very first one that ever was.

URSULA: It must be more than five thousand years old!

BASIL: It is. I dug it up near the Dead Sea, when I was looking for the ruins of Pompeii down there.

URSULA: Of… Pompeii…?

BASIL: Yes.

URSULA: Then…you're…you're an…an archaeologist…?

BASIL: Only in my spare time, I'm afraid, Ursula.

URSULA: Oh, Basil! Why did you never tell me? Why did you never tell me you were an archaeologist in your spare time?

BASIL: Would it have made so much difference?

URSULA: Oh, you dear, simple, foolish boy! Yes! It would have made all the difference…all the difference in the world!

BASIL: Darling.

URSULA: Tell me now. Tell me now that you're an archaeologist in your spare time.

BASIL: I've already told you, my angel.

URSULA: Tell me again. Let me hear you say it. Let me hear it from your own lips. Let me hear you say 'I am Sir Mortimer Wheeler's grandson!' …and be proud and strong and confident as the words ring out…!

BASIL: I am Sir Mortimer Wheeler's grandson.

URSULA: Oh, again! Again!

BASIL: I am Sir Mortimer Wheeler's grandson.

URSULA: Oh, Basil, my darling! Shall we go in? Shall we go in and…and do what…what comes naturally…? Say yes, Basil…please say Yes!

BASIL: Yes, Ursula…if that's what you wish.

URSULA: Oh, I do wish! I do wish! Come! Come now! I want it… I want it all…the sherds, the digs, the pottery, the…the carbon dating… I want it again and again…and again…

BASIL: I can't remember very much of it, my darling…

URSULA: What you can remember, then! *(Voice receding.)* Hurry…please hurry…!

BASIL: *(Following.)* I'll do my best, my darling but I'm very rusty…very rusty indeed.

Voices recede. A barely discernible, brief, discreet pause.

BASIL: I was less rusty than I thought I was, my darling.

URSULA: Oh, Basil…!

Fade.

Indefatigable in the pursuit of truth.

Oh, indeed.

Out in all weathers looking for it.

He's had the drains up more than once.

Here he comes now.

Any luck?

Hide nor hair.

N.F. Simpson (1919-2011) was a leading exponent of the Theatre of the Absurd, with the Royal Court classics *A Resounding Tinkle* (1957) and *One Way Pendulum* (1959) sealing his reputation as a comic master with a subtle philosophical undertow. Emerging during a revolutionary period in British theatre, Simpson rose to prominence alongside Harold Pinter, John Osborne and Arnold Wesker. His work has been embraced and performed by comedy legends including Spike Milligan, Eric Sykes, Beryl Reid and Dick Emery. His influence spread widely, from Peter Cook's much loved character E.L. Wisty to *Monty Python's Flying Circus*, and helped spawn a generation of outstanding comic talent. This authorised collection presents the best of Simpson's short works for audiences new and old. Featuring more than sixty pieces from across six decades, the full spectrum of an extraordinary career is brought together in one volume for the first time: monologues, sketches, criticism and poetry, written for radio, television, stage and print. It includes all of Simpson's anarchic collaborations with Willie Rushton for *Private Eye*, a generous selection of previously unseen pieces from his final manuscript, as well as a critical introduction by Simpson collaborator Simon Usher.